The beggar
was very na
learning to

The smart cat Olivia helped the princess make wise decisions for the kingdom.

The bad-tempered uncle, Lord Raisinkatz, threatened to *ZIGGLE AND TWIGGLE* anyone who made him angry.

The dutiful Sergeant Muster-Buster followed orders without thinking.

Tickory Tettle the Tax Collector traveled on his horse all the time and rolled off the horse just as many times.

The huntsman Na-Nicky calmly helped with the conflict and confusion found in the entire realm.

The Princess and the Beggar

Written and Illustrated
by
HARRY CHINCHINIAN

Edited by CAROLYN GRAVELLE

Published by Plum Tree Press, 531 Silcott Road, Clarkston, WA 99403.

Technical production and editing by Pine Orchard.
http://www.pineorchard.com

The author expresses special appreciation to Senior Editor Carolyn Gravelle.

Plum Tree Press titles are distributed and publicized by
Sheryn Hara & Company, P.O. Box 19732, Seattle, WA 98109.
(425) 775-7868

Library of Congress Catalog Card Number: 98-065251
ISBN 0-9653535-8-3

About the Heather and Holly Brown Series

Jo-Lo came into Heather Brown's life when she was eight years old and terribly lonely. It's not that she didn't have friends. She did. But, as you know, sometimes you can be *terribly* lonely, even when you're surrounded by lots and lots of people.

Jo-Lo stayed for several years because he and Heather had many adventures together, and enjoyed each other's company so very much. Whenever Heather wanted a story, Jo-Lo quickly obliged. *The Princess and the Beggar* is just one of his many stories.

Then, as suddenly as he appeared, Jo-Lo went away. Heather was miserable and kept calling for him to come back.

When he finally did return, after a week, he explained in his kindest way, that she really didn't need him anymore. Another eight-year-old girl was terribly lonely like she had been and this little girl needed him very badly, much more than Heather herself.

Jo-Lo pointed out to Heather that she was now sixteen, a young *adult* with a driver's license, swimming and soccer teammates, and plenty of school activities including (Jo-Lo smiled sadly as he said this) dancing with boys.

It wasn't until days after Jo-Lo had left that Heather thought it over carefully and agreed to let him go. But she could never forget Jo-Lo and their times together. Of course, Jo-Lo remains in a special part of Heather's heart forever.

As for Holly Brown, the mixed-up dragon named Dingle came into her life at the same time when she

was also eight years old. In the same way, it appears—as Holly takes more and more time with her horse shows, basketball games, swim meets, and chums—that her best friend Dingle will leave to keep company with another little girl or boy who needs him much more.

Foreword

My part, as the author, is to write down what happened to Heather and Holly Brown the few short years when they knew Jo-Lo and Dingle.

I'll try to be accurate when I write this. But it's not as easy as it sounds when Heather and Holly read everything recorded about them, and are very critical about the slightest mistake.

Luckily, their mother is more tolerant and even amused, which helps, because she understands all too well how confusing it is to keep track of Jo-Lo and Dingle when they are with these two girls.

This book *The Princess and the Beggar* is one of Jo-Lo's stories for Heather.

Harry Chinchinian

The Princess and the Beggar

"Good morning, Heather Brown."

Heather sat down and watched Jo-Lo settle himself around her feet. She softly stroked his head with her foot and sighed, "Good morning, Jo-Lo."

It was another cold, dark day in the fall when the leaves were turning colors, and she just didn't feel like doing anything at all. It was so pleasant just to sit and daydream out the window.

"Jo-Lo, tell me a story."

"Wouldn't you rather travel some place and see things?" asked Jo-Lo hopefully. "And we could take some cookies with us."

Heather suddenly jumped up, put her hands on her hips, and looked down at her tumbled-over friend. "Are you saying you want me to bake some cookies?"

"Me?" Jo-Lo acted astonished, picking himself up. "Did I say anything about wanting cookies?"

"Jo-Lo, say what you want," Heather insisted.

"Say what I want? Hmmm . . ." Jo-Lo paused as if he had to think hard about this. He placed his hand under his chin as though he were in deep thought. "Well, if we were to go anywhere or do anything, it would be really nice, I mean awfully nice, if somehow, someone, actually anyone, made something nourishing."

Jo-Lo twisted around, and placing his head on the floor, looked up at Heather with a crinkly smile.

She knew Jo-Lo would keep on teasing and teasing her until she made the cookies.

He started rolling on the floor, pulling up his ears. While saying, "Gug, gug, gug!" he put his paws in his mouth, pulled on the sides, made stupid faces, and shook so hard that Heather just saw teeth. He was so much like a child in so many ways.

"All right," Heather gave in.

"You will?" Jo-Lo stopped his antics. "I'll help you."

"No, no, no!" begged Heather. "I know all about the way you help. When you finish helping, there's nothing left to bake."

Heather went into the kitchen, got the ingredients, and began to soften the butter in the microwave. When she turned around, some of the chocolate chips were gone.

"Jo-Lo, you just ate half of the chocolate!"

"Me?" gulped Jo-Lo.

"Shame on you."

"Put in some raisins instead. Same thing, you know," mumbled Jo-Lo with his mouth still full.

"Raisins are not the same thing, and you know it. Now, stop!"

So Heather had to make half the batch with chocolate chips and a separate batch with raisins. She added nuts and oatmeal to both, and put them in the oven.

"Now, on with the story," she demanded with her part of the bargain done.

"Yeah, okay . . . once there was a princess—"

"Wait! It has to have a happy ending. And I don't want the story about the boy who found a big toe in his backyard, cooked it, and then ate it."

"How about the empty house that was guarded by a bloody head?" giggled Jo-Lo, smiling teasingly.

Heather glared. "You know stories like that keep me awake at night. No cookies for you!"

"Come to think of it," as he listened to his tummy growl, "the story about the princess and the beggar is something you'll like."

"Begin then!" ordered Heather firmly. She sat down, crossed her arms, and waited.

Jo-Lo sighed, lay down next to her, and covered one of Heather's feet with his front furry paws. He sniffed a few times to clear his nose and then began:

"Once upon a time there was—"

"Stop right there!" exclaimed Heather. "I don't like stories that begin that way."

"Well," repositioned Jo-Lo, "allow me to try again." He took a deep breath and began:

"There was once a beautiful girl who was to become queen upon her eighteenth birthday. She didn't know this because no one was allowed to tell her. You see, her father and mother were dead and she was being brought up by her nearest relative, an uncle, who people thought as a very selfish and wicked man."

"How wicked?"

"Well, he never went anywhere without his guards to do his bidding. He would order his sergeant to ZIGGLE AND TWIGGLE anyone who made him angry."

"What do you mean ZIGGLE AND TWIGGLE?" inquired Heather.

"What do you mean by asking what those words mean? If you don't know such simple things," sniffed Jo-Lo, "I might as well stop the story."

"You don't know either, do you?" suspected Heather.

Jo-Lo acted very hurt. "Of course, I do. I'm the one who's telling the story. Now how do you expect me to tell the story if you're going to constantly question me?"

With that, he got up and lay down in the corner, covering his head and ears with his paws.

Heather waited. The smell of baking cookies filled the room.

"I think I'll call Holly, Nathan, and Nicky to let them know that some freshly baked cookies are just out of the oven and are begging to be eaten," baited Heather.

Jo-Lo immediately jumped up, his pouting forgotten. "But the story. I promised you a story and I must keep my promise. But we must rescue the burning cookies. Yes, they're burning. I'm sure they are. Hurry!"

Heather smiled. "You stay here. I'll save the cookies. And while we eat them, you will continue the story and not get fussed up if I ask a simple question."

"Hurry," prompted Jo-Lo.

Heather brought out the two different kinds of cookies. After filling his mouth full, Jo-Lo began: "Once upon a time—"

"I told you not to begin that way! You already said there's a mean uncle who has an army and keeps the princess in the castle from knowing she's to become a queen. Now, go on."

Jo-Lo looked puzzled. "I don't remember saying he was mean and that she was hidden in a castle." Jo-Lo shook his head. "You're ahead of me, Heather. Should I tell a different story?"

"No, I want to hear this one, especially if it has a happy ending. It does have a happy ending, doesn't it?"

"Depends upon your point of view," Jo-Lo said

mysteriously, his eyebrows twitching from side to side. He then placed one raisin-nut cookie in one side of his mouth and cautioned, "Please do not . . . ," pausing to place a chocolate-chip cookie in the other side, "I repeat," chewing slowly, "do not interrupt the storyteller."

Heather said nothing.

Jo-Lo began:

1

Far, far away on top of the highest hill was the greatest stone castle. Princess Gwyn-o-cheri lived there.

Her father and mother, who were king and queen, died when she was too young to rule. So her wicked uncle, Lord Raisinkatz, became the temporary ruler of their kingdom.

Lord Raisinkatz made sure the castle doors were always guarded night and day, and that his servants were very careful to keep everything locked up tightly. At the edges of the kingdom, signs with "no trespassing" were clearly posted on every fence, and guardhouses and guards were stationed at entrances and exits everywhere.

Lord Raisinkatz found great joy in cruising around the boundaries of his land to make sure that no one dared trespass. He was always fond of saying, "SPECIAL PERMISSION IS REQUIRED," and then never giving it, "PERMISSION NOT GRANTED!"

He enjoyed giving orders, lots of them, and insisted they be obeyed immediately. His loyal army of men stayed close by to carry out all their lord's orders quickly and swiftly. If not, the soldiers feared being *ZIGGLED AND TWIGGLED*, something too awful to think about.

It was a horrible punishment which Lord Raisinkatz used, especially when he was displeased or out-of-sorts on a particular day. How did he learn about this unusual punishment? It was from a dozen wizards who were banished from every normal place in the realm. They were too cruel and dastardly for anyone to tolerate. But Lord Raisinkatz paid them many gold coins to figure out the worst of worst tortures. They came up with the scary and dreadful *ZIGGLE AND TWIGGLE*. When that happened, no one ever saw the person who was *ZIGGLED AND TWIGGLED* again!

Why didn't anyone leave this kingdom? Well, because citizens required special permission to leave, which—as you guessed it—was never granted!

Lord Raisinkatz never allowed calendars or clocks either. So no one ever knew the time. All the clocks were kept in his locked private room with their tick-tocks and gongs gone, buried beneath all the calendars that told the day of the week, the week of the month, the month of the year, and the year of the century.

Sometimes when it got too cold and was obviously winter, Lord Raisinkatz would decide it was summer and make everyone wear summer clothes. At other times (for the lord was easily bored) he would decide that summer was too hot and declare it to be winter, and then everyone was ordered to bundle up with their warmest clothes. Since the lord's word was law, no one dared complain, even though they shivered and caught terrible colds from the lack of clothes in the winter or suffered horrible heat strokes with the heavy clothes they were forced to wear in the hot summer.

It became even more difficult for the citizens when Lord Raisinkatz decreed that night was day and day was night. In fact, people couldn't even get out of bed until they heard the town crier's voice: "Arise, arise! It has been decreed by the great Lord Raisinkatz that it is daytime. Everyone rise and begin work!"

Of course, no one dared wonder why they were getting up at night or going to bed when the sun was at its peak during the day. They dared not question any of his rules since Lord Raisinkatz was the "Lord of the Land." And since only he could decide what manners were good and what manners were bad, he decreed, quite confidently, that his own manners were simply superb.

To make sure that the townspeople were truly obedient, Lord Raisinkatz planted spies everywhere and paid them quite well to report anyone who broke his rules.

Everybody lived in complete fear and began to speak only in whispers, even when no one was around to report what was said. Lord Raisinkatz liked hearing his people speak softly because his voice sounded so much better and more convincing, especially when he shouted. Soon Lord Raisinkatz only roared when he spoke. So he added to his 317 rules that everyone was required to whisper. Otherwise, they would be punished.

After many years of obeying and living in fear of being *ZIGGLED AND TWIGGLED*, the townspeople and almost all the others lost their normal voices and could not shout or yell, no matter how hard they tried. Even when foreigners came to visit, they began to whisper as well, not because they had to or wanted to, but because whispering was catching—something like yawning.

To sum it up then (if I can keep my voice down) it was Lord Raisinkatz's privilege and pride to create all the Rules of Conduct to make himself look mighty, mighty powerful.

2

Princess Gwyn-o-cheri refused to talk in a whisper. "I don't care."

"But it's not allowed, my lady," whispered her attendant.

"I don't care. I'm going out," replied the princess in a loud voice.

You see, Princess Gwyn-o-cheri was the only one allowed to speak as she wanted. But that was after Lord Raisinkatz raged at her for speaking with a normal voice and after her cat Olivia, in defense of the princess, slashed the bottom of his fine silk, purple jacket. Tearing the lord's jacket in long pieces was Olivia's warning of what could come. Since Lord Raisinkatz was still wearing the jacket, he decided to allow the princess to speak as she wanted. That decision came from the kindness of his proud heart and in the best interest of his many allergies.

Not only was Lord Raisinkatz allergic to dogs, horses, and plants of every kind, but he was especially allergic to cats. When he was around them, his huge nose began to run, and he would sneeze, cough, and gasp for air. That's why he always carried a handkerchief. And to avoid touching these terrible objects by mistake, he usually wore white gloves that he would change as soon as he saw the slightest spot of dirt or animal hair on them.

Unfortunately, Lord Raisinkatz, who had all these allergies, insisted that the sun would ruin the delicate, clear, white skin of the princess, and the outside air would ruin her delicate lungs. He commanded that Princess Gwyn-o-cheri remain within the castle at all times and never, but never, go outside.

"I've decided to go outside. Right now!" said Princess Gwyn-o-cheri to her lady attendant. "It is simply ridiculous that I am not allowed any sunshine or fresh air."

"Oh, no!" cried her attendant in a whisper.

"I am going to feel the sunshine on my skin, breathe

fresh air into my lungs, touch the green leaves on the trees and shrubs with my bare hands, and smell all the beautiful fresh flowers. Every single one of them!"

"It's not allowed, my lady. I'll be blamed for letting you . . ." The attendant paused as she thought about the penalty of very horrible things which are too horrible to think about or describe.

"Nonsense! It's my decision, not yours. I'm old enough to do what I want."

So before they could be stopped, the princess and Olivia slid down the outside garden railing, down to the ground, and by running quickly, were out of sight, covering a large distance from the greatest stone castle as only a young girl and cat could.

Soon, far away (but not that far away) she and Olivia were walking in the warm sunshine around the beautiful grounds which held crops and gardens. When they met two elderly people, the princess greeted them so pleasantly in a normal voice.

"Hello, you good people. It's such a lovely day today, isn't it?"

The old folks stopped working in the field and gaped, for they had never seen such a beautiful young girl. She had long golden hair, smooth white skin, such bright blue-gray eyes, and dressed so elegantly in soft silky pinks. Her melodious voice sounded like the finest flute in an orchestra.

"It has to be a dream," some whispered, "because not only is she beautiful but she speaks so clearly. She speaks above a whisper!"

As the princess continued her walk and spoke to others, many pinched themselves to be sure they were really awake. At first, they became frightened and thought they were seeing a wondrous vision with a white cat. They stared and stared, and some even crossed themselves. Could this be a sign of good fortune?

But back at the greatest stone castle, there was much commotion to be heard and seen. Orders were being given in the loudest of loud whispers.

"She has hidden somewhere. Look again!"

"She has fallen out of the window. Look below!"

"No, she's not there. Quick, call the sergeant and tell him. Or we'll be worse than fricasseed chicken."

The sergeant-in-charge, Sergeant Muster-Buster, began calling out commands: "Five of you soldiers, go up the draw. Five, check up and down the gully. Six, search the east, and five, follow the river. The rest of you, come with me."

The huge gates slowly creaked open, and a large group of men scurried out. Some ran on foot while others rode horses and mules. All of them went in different directions.

In the distance, Princess Gwyn-o-cheri and Olivia heard the noises from the greatest stone castle and knew what was happening. They decided to walk even faster and go farther away, perhaps hide if necessary, behind the many shrubs or in one of the many flower beds.

3

On the same bright, sunny day, a beggar seemed to somehow slip through the rusty, closed gates, where Lord Raisinkatz posted his Rules of Conduct. It was most unusual to have someone enter the gates, rather than try to leave, so the guards were slow to pay him any mind. Besides, the beggar acted quite harmless and was already down the path, heading toward town.

He walked with a smile as though he didn't have a care in the world. He played a harmonica and wore tattered clothes. Not an ordinary beggar, mind you, but someone who looked rather ordinary.

One guard, however, became a bit miffed at how easily the beggar had passed through by saying, "Hi, there. How's it goin', guys?"

So the guard thought he would have some fun scaring the stranger. He threw his spear just to see how close he could come without hitting the beggar. But hardly had he thrown the spear, when the spear turned into a fierce, black raven!

The bird then turned around, flew back at a very fast speed, and aimed its sharp beak right at the head of the cowardly guard.

You have to admit that the guard was a coward. After all, anyone who would throw a spear at a defenseless person is not brave.

The guard had to duck every which way while the raven dove at him over and over and over. Finally, he hid inside the guard station for protection.

His partner laughed and laughed, "Ha-ha-ha. Ho-ho-ho." He laughed so hard that he bent over to ease the pain the laughter had caused.

The cowardly guard got so angry at being laughed at that he began to run after the beggar to teach him a lesson (whatever that lesson might be).

But his partner grabbed his arm tightly, stopped laughing, and warned, "Be more than stupid. That one has powerful magic. If Lord Raisinkatz hears that we let in a magician, we'll be *ZZZZ . . . ZZZZI . . . ZZZZIG* . . . I can't bear to say it. Just forget what happened."

The cowardly guard thought only a moment and shuddered at how close he had come to such terrible punishment. "I've completely forgotten what happened!" the coward agreed. "Ever so completely, I have, I have."

Upon arriving in town, the beggar walked into Pinchdoodle Inn and ordered, of course, in a normal voice, "One mug of Fizzybrew, please."

"You're not from around here," whispered Innkeeper Pinchdoodle.

Looking around, the beggar whispered back (since whispering is contagious, you know), "How did you guess?"

Pinchdoodle looked closer at his customer and decided not to tell the truth. He squinted and whispered, "Your clothes, I guess. They make me think you're a stranger. They're different than what we normally wear."

The young stranger looked down at himself and saw tattered, patched clothes and shoes. "I hope they don't offend you."

"Certainly not," Pinchdoodle lied again.

"After all, they are clean." The beggar proudly brushed

his clothes with his hands as if he didn't tolerate the smallest of dust specks on them.

Shaking his head, the innkeeper reassured him, "Not offensive at all."

Pinchdoodle had so little business that he was careful not to discourage a paying customer. This customer could pay, couldn't he? Pinchdoodle knew he better find out now, so he demanded, "That'll be five dramkittles."

He kept his hand on the drink and his eye on the beggar.

The beggar couldn't believe his ears. "Five dramkittles for a simple brew to quench my thirst?"

Pinchdoodle said not a word as he pulled the drink closer to himself and farther from his customer. But when the beggar reached into his patched pocket, pulled out a coin, and placed it on the counter, the drink was his.

Pinchdoodle smiled at the pricey exchange.

"Rather expensive, is it not?" asked the beggar as he lifted the mug for a sip.

A clear, calm voice spoke behind the beggar. "Lord Raisinkatz would not like to hear you say that. The lord sets the prices and he always confiscates half."

"Confiscates half the price of the drink, you say?" The beggar turned to find himself speaking to a small, wiry man.

"No different than any other item that's sold here, where Raisinkatz rules," replied the man.

Outraged by this injustice, the beggar exclaimed, "What terrible taxation! You should rebel against it. Terribly selfish, I must say." The beggar reached into his pocket and began to play a slow, sad tune on his harmonica.

Pinchdoodle stole into the back room. Someone was being sent to report the beggar's words to Lord Raisinkatz. Such outbursts would insure a person to be *ZZZ . . . ZIGGLED . . .*

Fearfully looking around, the little man warned the beggar, "You must get out of here! Quickly!"

"I'm afraid of no one," declared the beggar. "Let come what may."

He began to play a much happier tune on his harmonica and much louder than before.

"Oh, no! I should have expected this," the little man said to himself. "His whole family is stubborn. All the sons leave home without anything but four coins and want to make their way in the world. I'll do what I can to help."

The small, wiry man quickly slipped out the side door and left.

4

Hardly had the beggar finished a half swallow of his Fizzybrew while playing a drinking song on his harmonica, when a dozen guards clumped into Pinchdoodle Inn. Swords and spears were shining brightly.

"Where is he, Pinchdoodle?" whispered Sergeant Muster-Buster who tried barking the question as loudly as he could. His whole body quivered. His chest decorations jingled and glistened with authority in the subdued light from the windows.

"There! He's the one!" the innkeeper gleefully whispered. He pointed to the only other person in the inn. "I get the reward for this, you know. I reported him. Don't forget, I get the reward." He rubbed his greedy hands together.

"Reward? Reward? Here's your reward, buster." Sergeant Muster-Buster reached for a dagger and threw it to pin Pinchdoodle to the wall by his shirt. "You low-down tattletale, everyone hates a tattletale!"

Pinchdoodle quavered, "It's just that . . . I could use the money. It would be nice to have some money, you know. Fix the place up or something. Make it look nice—"

Sergeant Muster-Buster was not sympathetic and not interested in reasons. In military fashion, he explained, "Tattletales used to receive rewards. But no longer. Lord Raisinkatz changed his mind about that as of four moments ago."

The sergeant would have said "four minutes ago" or

“four hours ago” or “four months ago” but he wasn’t allowed a watch or to even know what exactly made up a minute, an hour, a month, or for that matter, even a year.

CRASH!

Fourteen glasses fell from the shelves and shattered as Pinchdoodle freed himself from the dagger which held his shirt to the wall. The shirt had torn in three places before he got loose. He held up the torn pieces and stared at them. He’d have to buy a new shirt too.

“You there, buster!” ordered Sergeant Muster-Buster. “Stranger, who insults the Lord Raisinkatz. Come with us, unless you want to die right here!”

“Whatever amuses you,” replied the beggar, continuing to play his harmonica. The soldiers began to listen to his music and smile and nod their heads in rhythm. It was very good music, good dancing music at that, certainly not the kind to muster to.

“Whatever amuses me? Amuses me, you say?” Sergeant Muster-Buster reached for his spear and threw it at the beggar, expecting to pin him against the table for such an impertinent reply.

Pinchdoodle smiled and giggled.

But Sergeant Muster-Buster missed. He never missed his target! How could this be?

Angry at missing such an easy target, especially in front of his men (who should be mustered) Sergeant Muster-Buster whipped out his sword and slashed at the beggar, slashing just lightly, just enough to tear his clothes, just enough to scare him.

Again, the edge of his sword seemed to just barely

miss each and every time. Miss and miss and miss.

Swish! Swish! Swish!

The swishing sound of the sword echoed and re-echoed in the room like a wind whistling through a hole in the window.

A clear, calm voice sounded from the entrance of the inn. "Sergeant."

Sergeant Muster-Buster paused to look over. There in the pale light stood a small, wiry man, leaning against the door with his hands in his pockets, shaking his head.

"What do you want, buster? You are interfering with my duties. Do you want a taste of this blade, too?" The sergeant was so furious at missing the beggar with his weapons that he made a move towards the little man. But the man sadly pointed to the sergeant's sword and ducked out the door once again.

Sergeant Muster-Buster looked to see what the man had pointed at and held up his trusty sword. No wonder the soldiers were laughing.

His sword was a cornstalk!

He had been swinging and jabbing with a cornstalk. What happened to his sword? In frustration and confusion, the sergeant threw it down. He had to get on with his duties.

Mustering up as much military composure as he could, Sergeant Muster-Buster shouted in his loudest whisper: "Out! Move'm out! We're going to the castle so this strange beggar-buster can be dealt with by Lord Raisinkatz."

But by now, the voice of Sergeant Muster-Buster was less confident. He knew that the cornstalk meant something. He wasn't sure what it was. But when he had time, he would think on it and sort it all out. Later, that is, when he had more time.

The beggar allowed the soldiers to move him outside. Six soldiers mustered in front of him and six marched behind. As they moved along the street, the beggar spotted the greatest stone castle on the highest hill. "Is that the castle where someone has hidden the most beautiful princess in the entire kingdom?"

"That's none of your business, you jobless buster," said the sergeant, trying to take charge again.

"Isn't her name Gwyn-o-pear? Gwyn-o-grape? Gwyn-o-something? What is it?"

"We don't answer questions from lice-ridden busters. The powerful Lord Raisinkatz commands that we bring lawbreakers to him. And we obey. Move. Or we'll exterminate you on the spot!"

After saying that, Sergeant Muster-Buster had a terrible thought. He stopped the march just as they were crossing a bridge, and began to inspect the beggar's hair and clothes. It wouldn't do to bring lice into the greatest stone castle now, would it? He shuddered at what would happen to him if he did that.

So the beggar was searched as he patiently leaned against the wooden bars of the bridge. While the sergeant was examining his clothes, the beggar began to play a very handsome march that made the guards perk up and, in spite of their wishes, caused them to stamp their feet very smartly.

Stomp! Stomp! Stomp!

Unfortunately, as they stamped in rhythm to the music, eight of the wooden planks supporting the floor of the bridge broke. Six soldiers fell into the water below.

Plop. Plop. Plop. Plop. Plop. Ker-plop!

Sergeant Muster-Buster looked down at his men swimming in the river with great surprise. The stomp-stomp's became ker-ploppity-plop's.

"What clumsy clods! They'll have to catch up as best they can. March on without them!" he ordered as the remaining soldiers mustered in formation.

But the beggar changed his musical marching tune and soon after he did, a swarm of large insects buzzed around the soldiers to annoy them.

Buzz, buzz, buzz.

The buzzing sounds became louder and louder.

BUZZ! BUZZ!

But worse, the stings were sharp and painful.

"Ow!" screamed one soldier after another. "Ow, ow!"

A few ran off and others jumped into the river with those who had stomp-stomped and ker-ploppity-plopped. All of them, however, ducked under the water to avoid the wrath of the buzzing, stinging insects.

Sergeant Muster-Buster ignored the insects, even when they stung. You could tell he had earned his sergeant's rank by never neglecting his duty, in spite of pain and discomfort. Pride of duty and obeying commands in all things, without question, were his job. Slandering his lord's name was against the law and it was his duty to arrest all individuals, like the beggar, who broke the law. As the sergeant continued to ignore the increasing stinging pain and kept guarding his prisoner, the beggar began playing a different tune.

The buzzing, stinging insects disappeared as quickly as they came.

"Are you all right?" asked Sergeant Muster-Buster. "It is my sworn duty to protect you until we dispose of you in some unmentionably painful manner."

The beggar merely nodded and smiled.

"Something's wrong," muttered Sergeant Muster-Buster to himself. "Something is quite different about all this. I must think on this and sort all this out as soon as I have time. Yes, that's what I'll do. Sort it all out as soon as I have more time."

Having made what he considered a very wise decision, Sergeant Muster-Buster, with military pride, continued on to Lord Raisinkatz's castle with the beggar as his prisoner.

5

"AM I UNHAPPY? DOES ANYONE CARE TO ASK?" Lord Raisinkatz shouted in his normal manner at Sergeant Muster-Buster who had just come in with the prisoner.

"Are you unhappy, my lord?" whispered the sergeant, all in the line of duty.

"UNHAPPY? MY CAREFULLY CONSIDERED ANSWER IS IN ONE WORD. THE WORD, AND I HOPE I DON'T SURPRISE YOU," responded Lord Raisinkatz as he nervously paced back and forth, "IS . . . YES!" His potato face turned tomato-red as he repeated, "YES, YES, YES!"

"Yes, your lordship," nodded the sergeant in agreement.

"A SINGLE WORD BUT MEANINGFUL ONLY TO THOSE WHO ARE NOT COMPLETE NINCOMPOOPS!"

"Nincompoops, your lordship."

"MEANINGFUL ONLY TO THOSE WHO ARE NOT LILTING, LOONEY LUNATICS WITH BEETLES LOOSELY BOUNCING AROUND IN THEIR BRAINS!"

"Looney lunatics, your lordship."

"FIFTY SOLDIERS TO FIND ONE FORLORN, LOST LITTLE PRINCESS. WHAT IS THIS WORLD COMING TO? WHAT IS HAPPENING TO THE EFFICIENCY OF MY ORDER AND DOMAIN?"

Sergeant Muster-Buster looked down at his feet and

didn't reply.

Lord Raisinkatz turned to face the sergeant. "SOME HEADS NEED ROLL OFF THEIR BODIES, MUSTER-BUSTER. COMPLETELY OFF! MAKE A NOTE OF THAT."

"Yes, your lordship," responded the sergeant and he whipped out a notebook to write it down. He wondered if the last word was spelled b-o-d-y-s or b-o-d-i-e-s. But this was the wrong time to ask, so he wrote down both spellings to find out later, when he had more time.

Suddenly Lord Raisinkatz bent at the waist and pointed to his sergeant, "AND WHY ARE YOU BOTHERING ME AT A MOMENT LIKE THIS WITH A VERMIN-LADEN, FILTHY BEGGAR WHO—"

"He's not filthy, your lordship. Not really. I checked just before we marched in here." Sergeant Muster-Buster proudly whispered, "For lice, too."

"DON'T INTERRUPT ME AND MY THOUGHTS!" exclaimed Lord Raisinkatz, shouting at the top of his lungs. "YOU KNOW HOW I FORGET WHAT I'M GOING TO SAY WHEN I'M INTERRUPTED. HOW MANY TIMES MUST I TELL YOU? SAY YOU'RE SORRY."

"Sorry, my lord."

"THAT'S BETTER."

"Begging your pardon, my lord."

"MUCH BETTER."

Lord Raisinkatz raised his eyebrows, pulled at his gloves, flicked off a piece of lint, then blew into his handkerchief. "NOW, WHAT WAS I GOING TO SAY?" He glared at his sergeant.

"Not to bother you with a vermin-laden—" offered

Sergeant Muster-Buster.

"RIGHT! PUT HIM AWAY IN THE DUNGEON UPSTAIRS. I'LL DEAL WITH HIM LATER. AFTER MY MOST IMPORTANT PROBLEM IS TAKEN CARE OF."

"Excuse me, my lord. The dungeon is in the basement. We don't have any dungeon upstairs . . ." The sergeant paused for the explosion of words, knowing what was going to come.

"I KNOW THAT, SERGEANT. DON'T DO AS I SAY! DO AS I THINK. I MEAN DO AS I MEAN TO SAY, NOT WHAT I SAY! ARE YOU CLEAR AS TO WHAT I WANT? OR DO I APPOINT SOMEONE ELSE TO YOUR HIGH POST OF RESPONSIBILITY?"

"I understand completely, my lord. Perfectly, my lord.

It will be done as you know . . . say . . . mean . . . think to mean to say, my lord," placated the sergeant.

"FINALLY!" shouted Lord Raisinkatz extra loudly, for he had warmed up his voice enough now to truly enjoy both the sound and the satisfying vibrations of his vocal chords. "TRUE COMMUNICATION IS OFTEN SO VERY DIFFICULT."

"Yes, indeed," whispered the lord's attendants.

"WHAT WAS THAT YOU SAID? I COULDN'T HEAR IT."

"Yes, indeed," they all whispered ever so louder.

"THANK YOU," smiled Lord Raisinkatz, satisfied that there was some appreciation for true communication in his land.

Just then, the princess walked in with an escort of weary soldiers. Lord Raisinkatz leapt into the air, and spun around and around with joy.

"THERE YOU ARE, MY DEAR! HOW LOVELY YOU LOOK. EVEN WITH THOSE AWFUL ROSY-RED CHEEKS AND THAT HEALTHY SUNSHINE GLOW TO YOUR FACE!"

Lord Raisinkatz swiftly spun around again, changed his expression by narrowing his eyes and bending at the waist, glared at his assembled attendants with a warning. "THE NEXT TIME PRINCESS GWYN-A-CHERI ESCAPES, I SHALL DEAL HARSHLY WITH SOMEONE HERE. RIGHT HERE IN THIS VERY ROOM."

There was total silence.

"AM I BEING UNDERSTOOD?"

There was no answer.

"AM I COMMUNICATING?"

Still there was no answer.

"YES IS THE CORRECT ANSWER."

Lord Raisinkatz rubbed his hands together, snapped his fingers, and jigged around at the delightful thought of what he would do if they didn't agree with him.

The assembled attendants all whispered in a chorus: "Yes, my lord."

Princess Gwyn-o-cheri stamped her foot. "It's no one's fault that I escaped. You can't hold anyone responsible for my escaping, but me." And she stamped her foot again.

Not to be outdone, the cat Olivia lifted up her paw, waved it in the air, and snarled in her meanest manner.

M-E-OWWW! "You make this place a prison."

Then Olivia turned her back and strutted out, without asking the lord's permission.

Intrigued with the princess, Lord Raisinkatz ignored Olivia's rude departure. He studied the beauty of Princess Gwyn-o-cheri and commented, "YOU LOOK VERY FETCHING, PRINCESS, WHEN YOU ARE ANGRY. ENOUGH TO BE SOMEONE'S BRIDE!"

Oh, how everyone gasped! No one married in the entire kingdom until a person was old enough.

The Supreme King of All the Kingdoms, King Dinwiddley, refused to allow it. And everyone knew that Princess Gwyn-o-cheri was not of age to be married.

Irritated, Lord Raisinkatz pulled at his gloves. "YOU GASP? YOU BELIEVE SHE IS NOT YET OF AGE? WELL, SINCE I HAVE BEEN PLACED IN CHARGE OF TIME AND DATES, I HEREBY DECREE THAT PRINCESS GWYN-O-CHERI IS OF AGE TO MARRY AS OF . . . YES, YES, . . . RIGHT NOW!"

The lord smiled, so pleased with himself that he spun around and around. He threw both arms in the air, dancing with joy.

"Hey," a voice sounded out. "Hey, you can't make people older than what they are just by saying they are."

The attendants and soldiers were stunned with fear as they looked around to find who said those words. Lord Raisinkatz couldn't believe his ears. In anger, he spun around once again. "WHO DARES QUESTION MY WORD?"

"I do!" answered the beggar.

"I DARE SAY, OBVIOUSLY YOU ARE SOMEONE WHO NEEDS TO BE *ZIGGLED AND TWIGGLED!*"

The beggar smiled and acted very unconcerned as if to say, "So what? Who cares?"

"*ZIGGLE AND TWIGGLE* HIM ON THE SPOT! RIGHT NOW!" ordered Lord Raisinkatz. His potato head

with the tomato-red face turned beetle-blue and puggy-purple. "I, LORD RAISINKATZ, COMMAND THAT THE *ZIGGLE AND TWIGGLE* PUNISHMENT BE EXECUTED."

The lord drew his sword from its scabbard, pointed it at the beggar, and shouted: "*ZIGGLE AND TWIGGLE* HIM NOW!"

6

A clear, calm voice arrested Lord Raisinkatz's command like the soft sound of flying emu wings. "A moment of your time, if you please, your ever-most-sainted lordship."

"WHO SPEAKS NOW?" The lord was spinning around again in his royal robes.

"I speak, my lord," the voice spoke clearly and calmly.

"WHO DARES INTERRUPT—"

"I do, my lord," the voice interrupted calmly.

Lord Raisinkatz saw a small, wiry man who owned

the clear, calm voice. "I KNOW YOU! YOU'RE NA-NICKY THE HUNTSMAN."

"Yes, my lord, I am."

Na-Nicky deeply bowed in acknowledgment and with dignity.

"BUT I KNOW YOU NOT YET WELL ENOUGH TO DISLIKE YOU. HURRY UP AND SAY SOMETHING SO I CAN FIND A REASON TO *ZIGGLE AND TWIGGLE* YOU AS WELL!" Lord Raisinkatz wiggled his hips in delight.

"Better that I whisper to your ears alone, my lord."

"BETTER, YOU SAY? OR WORSE?"

"Much better," Na-Nicky emphasized clearly and calmly.

"MUCH BETTER? INDEED, IT MUST NEED BE MUCH BETTER, OR YOU TOO WILL VANISH FROM THE FACE OF THE EARTH FOREVER AND EVER!"

So Lord Raisinkatz and Na-Nicky held a conference, and everyone strained to listen.

Everyone could hear their lord very well, for his voice box had been forced to use the shouting portion for such a long time that the whisper section had withered away.

"REALLY? YOU DON'T SAY? DUKES AND . . .

WELL, WELL, WELL." Lord Raisinkatz glared at everybody so close by and declared, "NOTHING HAS BEEN SAID OR DONE THAT CAN CHANGE MY MIND. NOTHING!"

The people didn't move.

Lord Raisinkatz cleared his throat, glared some more, and declared again, "IT WILL BE JUST AS I SAID!"

No one moved.

He then blew into his white handkerchief, nervously wiped his red nose, straightened his shoulders, lifted his chin, and in a stately manner pointed out: "DUE TO CERTAIN CIRCUMSTANCES SEEMINGLY NOT COMPLETELY UNDER MY DOMINANCE, I SHALL DEFER, WHICH IS TO SAY GRANT, AN EXTENSION OF TIME THROUGH MY ROYAL KINDNESS, WHICH IS TO SAY THAT THE BEGGAR DOES NOT DIE NOW. NOT RIGHT AWAY. AT LEAST NOT YET." Lord Raisinkatz wiped the tears from his eyes with his purple sleeve.

Everyone was moved. Everyone sighed.

Na-Nicky smiled as he left the room.

Exhausted, Lord Raisinkatz collapsed into a soft chair, holding his head. He reflected out loud, "IT HAS BEEN A TIRESOME, TIRESOME DAY. I NEED TONIGHT TO THINK OF AN APPROPRIATE PUNISHMENT." He sighed with little movement.

As the lord was speaking, the beggar's eyes met those of the princess and something terribly important passed between them that is beyond any description for mere words. But it was close to a sudden electric shock, if an electric shock can ever be pleasant.

All this happened in the splittest of split seconds.

It happened between two people who couldn't explain it themselves. Except to say, it was a glowing feeling that each was meant for the other and that somehow, sometime, they would be together forever and ever and ever.

That's why the beggar's mouth dropped open as he gasped at the strength of this lightning blitz and understood its meaning.

At the same time, the princess noticed that her knees became suddenly very weak, and strange things began to happen to her heart.

Love at first sight has a way of doing things like that to people. Good manners are forgotten, and caution is tossed away like yesterday's dried-out macaroni.

The beggar had never before felt his mouth drop open like that in polite company, and as for the princess, she had never felt such a failing weakness in her knees as she barely caught herself from falling down.

Lord Raisinkatz interrupted their mutually surprised thoughts. His face was becoming beetle-red and puggy-night-purple and even slimy charcoal-green. "GET THAT CAT OUT OF HERE! RIGHT NOW!"

Everyone looked down to see what his finger was pointing at.

7

There it was. A large black tomcat who, seeing he had everyone's attention, puffed out his chest and very arrogantly walked over to snuggle against Princess Gwyn-o-cheri's collapsing knees. She promptly picked the cat up and held him protectively in her arms.

"No!" said the princess. "He is one of my cats!"

Lord Raisinkatz began to sneeze and sneeze and sneeze.

ACHOO! ACHOO! ACHOO! "I'M ALLERGIC TO CATS!"

The beggar cleared his throat and looked very solemn. "So there you are, Jasper Bartholomew!" he said, knowing his cat hated his middle name Bartholomew.

The beggar lifted Jasper from the princess' arms.

The tomcat looked at the beggar through half-closed

eyes. "Indeed, it's about time you found me. Are you ready to apologize?"

"For what? You didn't leave any clues. How would I know where to look for you?" asked the beggar.

"If you had studied your lessons harder instead of playing on that dreadful harmonica, you would have learned to be a better wizar—be smarter," exclaimed Jasper as he quickly changed his words.

Lord Raisinkatz listened to their exchange and found an excuse to shout at the beggar. "THAT'S YOUR CAT? NAMED JASPER BARTHOLOMEW? IS THAT HIS NAME? I DEMAND THAT CAT BE EXTERMIN—"

ACHOO! "EXTERM—"

ACHOO! "EX—"

ACHOO!

Lord Raisinkatz decided to forget the cat. Things were getting too much out of hand and, after all, this was his castle.

"YOU RAGGED WRETCH OF A BEGGAR," he shouted. "STOP STARING AT MY BEAUTIFUL NIECE, PRINCESS GWYN-A-CHERI. AND DO CLOSE YOUR MOUTH. SHE IS MINE TO MARRY TO WHOMEVER AND WHENEVER I PLEASE. DO NOT GAZE, GAWK, OR VIEW, UNLESS YOU HAVE MY SPECIAL

PERMISSION, WHICH IS NEVER GRANTED. TAKE HIM AWAY, SERGEANT. TO THE UPSTAIRS DUNGEON!"

Sergeant Muster-Buster quickly nodded. "Yes, indeed, your lordship. To the dungeon . . . upstairs."

"AS FOR YOU, YOU MISERABLE BAD LUCK CAT, I'LL DEAL WITH YOU LATER. AFTER I CAN THINK OF A SUITABLE, GRUESOME, AND GRISLY DEATH. BUT FIRST, I HAVE TO HAVE MY MEDICINE," wheezed Lord Raisinkatz. He strode off, using handkerchiefs in both hands to hold down the sneezing and sputtering and coughing.

As the sergeant started to hurry the beggar off, Jasper Bartholomew jumped into the arms of the princess and purred from his comfortable place. "Enjoy your restful place, beggar-man. Don't you just wish you could be where I am?"

"You're a naughty, naughty cat," scolded the beggar, envious of Jasper's place. "I don't know why I ever worried about you."

"The best always deserves the best," smiled Jasper, looking extremely satisfied with himself as he snuggled even deeper into the arms of the beautiful princess.

8

Sergeant Muster-Buster hurried the beggar down the cold stone steps to the damp, wet basement. It was a long way down.

"I'm hungry, sergeant. Don't you feed your prisoners?"

"Aye, that we do. But in your case, why does it matter? You are to be alive only until morning and it'll only be a waste of good food."

They walked past the steps of the basement and gazed into the deep hole in the ground which was the lord's dungeon.

"Am I to go way down there?" asked the beggar. He took a closer look. "Why, it's nothing but a deep, deep dirt hole. It looks pretty scary."

"Yes, indeed. That's the lord's dungeon."

"Have you ever been in there before, sergeant?" The beggar took another look. "What's it like down there?"

"How would I know what's it like down there? I'm a sergeant, not a prisoner."

"Sergeant, with all due respect, I'd just as soon not be down there." The beggar backed away from the hole. "I'd much rather spend the night between some clean sheets on a bed. Even some warm, clean straw in a barn would do."

"Ho! Clean sheets is it? Warm straw? Let me help you enjoy your sweet dreams, buster. Right now!" And with that, the sergeant poked the beggar hard with his spear, trying to push him toward the dungeon. Instead of poking the prisoner as he intended, Sergeant Muster-Buster was tickling him!

"Stop that," the beggar giggled. "That tickles."

The sergeant looked dumbfounded and shook what he held in his hand. His spear was no longer a spear. It had become a stalk of wilted celery. He was poking the prisoner with celery leaves!

The sergeant smelled it. Then he bit and tasted it to be sure. Celery!

The sergeant knew that when something felt like celery, looked like celery, smelled and tasted like celery, then it had to be celery.

Something foul had occurred. It was like the time in the inn when his spear turned into a cornstalk. He threw the celery into the dungeon with disgust.

"Behave yourself and act like a proper prisoner!" he shouted in a whisper at the beggar. "Jump into that deep, ugly, miserable dungeon like I order you to do."

The prisoner shook his head as he gazed back into

the black pit. "I'd really just as soon not. Especially since you have never been down there, and can't recommend it one way or another."

The sergeant understood insubordination when he heard it and this was a prime example of disobeying. He felt justified in using physical force, so he made a grab for the beggar to throw him in. Unfortunately, he wasn't watching his footing, for he slipped on the crumbling dirt and the sergeant tumbled

down,

down,

down

into the bottom of the deep dungeon.

9

Several moments passed before the sergeant realized what had happened. He had to wait until after the dirt and rocks stopped raining down on his head in order to speak. "Help me out of here, beggar-buster. Now!"

"But, Sergeant Muster-Buster," the beggar hollered down, "you just now got in."

"I know that, and now I want out. Now! That's an order."

"But you yourself just said that you hadn't tried this before. Why don't you see how comfortable it is . . . or isn't? That way, the next time you are asked, you can speak with authority about what it's like down there."

"No one is supposed to like a dungeon, beggar. Everyone knows that. It's punishment is what it is."

"But I don't recall doing anything to be punished for."

"Orders," cried the sergeant in his loudest whisper. "You heard them yourself. My orders were that you are to go into the dungeon."

With that, the beggar sat down on the edge of the hole and pulled out his harmonica to play a tune in order to think. He stopped, rather alarmed, and looked down to ask the sergeant, "You're just obeying orders without thinking? Now stop and think. What exactly did I do to deserve a punishment?"

"Orders are orders," whispered up the sergeant. "I don't have to think. Soldiers just obey orders."

Standing back up, the beggar finished his tune abruptly. "In that case, if you refuse to think on what I've done to deserve a punishment, you need to call and order someone else to help you out." With that, he played one long, last note and put the harmonica back into his patched pocket.

"But no one can hear me! The reason the dungeon is put way down here is that no one can hear the terrible crying and wailing of the prisoners. How can my soldiers help me if they can't hear me?" the sergeant moaned.

The beggar sat back down on the edge of the dungeon, dangled his legs over it, and reached into his knapsack. He brought out a chicken leg, an apple, and a large berry tart.

"You do have a problem that will require some thought, sergeant. But I'm so hungry. I hope you won't be offended if I take time to eat."

The sergeant looked up at the food and drooled. He had not eaten all day because of the early morning search for the princess and then rushing to town to arrest the beggar for his unlawful remarks against the lord.

"You're eating the tart first," sulked the sergeant, his voice bouncing off the wall of the dungeon, sounding hollow. He scolded, "You're not allowed to do that!"

"Indeed," said the beggar coolly, "and pray tell, who made it a rule that you cannot eat dessert first?"

"It just isn't done. You're not allowed to do that. Everyone knows that."

"Tell me, sergeant, would you like to eat a tart first?"

"Well, yes."

"Even though you're not supposed to do so?"

"Yes, but I never do. Because I've been taught to eat properly and that means eating things that are good for you first."

Just the same, the sergeant's eyes fastened on the tart and the more he saw the juice running down the sides of the pastry, the hungrier he became. His mouth kept filling up with saliva. He had to swallow and swallow to get rid of it.

He felt in his pockets and looked around the dungeon, then spotted the stalk of wilted celery which he had thrown in. It was now covered with dirt and twigs. He picked it up, brushed it off as best he could, and took a bite.

"I've always hated celery," he mumbled under his breath and looked up very sadly. "Always."

The beggar had a soft heart. He divided up the tart and threw half down to the sergeant who had trouble to keep from gobbling it up too fast.

While the beggar and sergeant ate, they heard a clear, calm voice.

"Hello, there. Am I interrupting anything?"

It was Na-Nicky the Huntsman.

10

"You're welcome to supper, even though we've already begun eating," invited the beggar.

"I bet you ate the best part first," sighed Na-Nicky. "You always did as a young'un."

"Yes, he did," complained the sergeant from the dungeon. "And he made me do it too. Because it looked so good!"

"Yes, well, he hasn't changed a bit since he was a child." Na-Nicky then turned to the beggar and asked, "So, what are your plans now?"

“I have no plans really,” said the beggar, “except to play a tune on my harmonica now and then.” With that, the beggar began to play.

“May I suggest something, if it does not give offense?”

“Certainly,” said the beggar, stopping his tune to answer.

“Well, then . . . ” Na-Nicky stepped closer to the dirt hole. “Sergeant, you’re still down there, aren’t you?” Na-Nicky wanted his attention too. “I suggest a trade. The beggar will give you half his food if you will change clothes with him.”

Sergeant Muster-Buster was a big man who needed lots of food to carry on his work. He was too hungry to refuse and ask why. The more he looked at the celery stalk, the more the wilted vegetable seemed to laugh at him. The morsel of tart he just ate only increased his hunger. He knew it was wrong to give up his clothes but, he told himself, the other soldiers would come down soon and he’d only be trading for a short time.

The sergeant agreed.

The beggar removed his ragged clothing and rolled them into a bundle. He took a piece of strong string from his knapsack and tied it around the bundle, then lowered it into the deep, deep dungeon.

Very slowly and unhappily, the sergeant took his uniform off and tied it to the string which the beggar pulled back up.

The sergeant found the beggar’s clothes were not a bad fit. The beggar was larger than he appeared, and the clothes were very comfortable.

“Here comes the beginning of our food bargain,”

announced the beggar. He lowered some bread into the dungeon. After that, he bit into the chicken leg and saved exactly half for the sergeant. He then ate half an apple and gave the sergeant the rest.

"By the way," inquired the beggar of Na-Nicky, "you said you knew me as a child."

"Yes, I was employed by your father as a huntsman many years ago and it remains my duty to look out for the son of my former master. So here I am."

"Well, my friend Na-Nicky, what do you suggest I do now?"

Na-Nicky shrugged. "It's late. The sergeant always retires early because he has to be up mustering his men and marching around before dawn. I shall be happy to show you where he sleeps."

"In that case, I'm off to sleep in the sergeant's quarters and to sleep between clean sheets."

Pleased with these results, the beggar quickly brushed all the dirt off his new clothes and polished the awards on the sergeant's uniform that jingled and tinkled when the medals struck each other.

Muster-Buster acted like a typical prisoner by scowling and gnashing his teeth, groaning (of course, always in a whisper) and pounding on the sides of the dungeon. But stop he soon did, for too much dirt and too many rocks kept falling and rolling down on him.

Besides, no one could hear him and he was very, very tired.

11

The next morning, after a refreshing sleep, the beggar yawned and looked out the window of his room.

What had happened to him? He had come to get his cat but now he had no desire to leave, even though Lord Raisinkatz had threatened his life. It bothered him that Jasper Bartholomew was being comfortably cuddled in the arms of Princess Gwyn-o-cheri. His jaw began uncontrollably twitching at the thought. The more he thought of it, the more . . . . Perhaps, if he became a cat. No, that wouldn't be fair play for a wizard—even an amateur one, like himself.

Maybe he should rest somewhere and get his muddled mind unmuddled from the electricity that had bonded him in some way to the beautiful princess. Maybe it was a one-time thing and wouldn't happen again.

He was a bit embarrassed to admit that his cat felt he was not getting enough treats and had run away, refusing to stay with him. How do you convince a cat that goodies are only for now and then? Especially a cat like Jasper who didn't like criticism of any kind at any time?

"Sergeant!"

The beggar whipped around.

"What are the orders for this morning?" asked a guard.

The beggar rubbed his sleepy eyes, trying to gain time while he thought. He was hungry. "Bring me some breakfast right away and send some down to the poor beggar of a prisoner after I've finished."

"Yes, sir."

The guard saluted, clicked his boots together, then turned on his heels smartly, and went to obey the commands.

"Well," thought the beggar to himself, "this could be a neat place to stay after all."

Hardly had the breakfast been brought, when Jasper Bartholomew squeezed through the door, hopped up on the table, and began picking out what he wanted to eat. He didn't bother with a greeting.

"I see you haven't changed your ways, naughty cat."

"And why should I?" grinned Jasper.

A loud, high-pitched voice cut through their conversation. "Jasper!"

Both Jasper and the beggar jumped at the sound to see who it was.

A beautiful, large, white, female cat with angry blue eyes was at the doorway. She was furious! "Is this the way you begin your day? By leaving your family without breakfast? Eating breakfast by yourself with a stranger?" She hissed.

For the first time since he had known Jasper, the beggar saw his cat look embarrassed and cowered down.

"I'm sorry, my dear," apologized Jasper.

"Dear?" wondered the beggar. "Jasper had called someone dear?"

"This is my beloved master. I haven't seen him for a long time and was overcome with emotion to see him," Jasper explained.

"Master?" asked Olivia. "And you haven't bothered to introduce us?"

"Olivia, this is my master. Master, this is Olivia."

"How do you do," bowed the beggar politely.

"How-do-you-do, indeed!" said Olivia not a bit mollified. "You two take your breakfast up to our room and eat with us. Right now!" She turned and glared at the beggar. "And what kind of manners did you teach your cat that allows him to simply walk off at breakfast time and eat all by himself without the slightest thought of others?"

"Others?" wondered the beggar. "There are others? What others?"

He tried to catch the eye of Jasper but it was no use. Jasper had scurried down and was following Olivia, knowing full well that the beggar would follow as he had been directed.

12

The beggar, dressed in the sergeant's clothes, picked up the tray of food before he realized that sergeants don't carry such things. It was against some very strict officer code. Men of rank only carry doohickeys such as swords and spears and maces. But not trays of food.

"Soldier!" he called outside the door. "Carry this breakfast tray to wherever Olivia orders—I mean, wherever those two cats are going."

The soldier was surprised. But then, a sergeant was a sergeant and orders were orders. So he traipsed behind the cats, up the long staircase, past all the large, heavy doors to the one door at the end of the hallway that had a guard posted outside.

"Sergeant says to bring this here."

The guard saluted and allowed him to pass. The soldier set the breakfast tray on the table and left.

Hardly had he gone when five kittens leapt from

a hiding place under the bed and began eating as though they had never seen food before.

"They're so hungry! How did you expect me to feed them all by myself?" asked Olivia, looking at Jasper crossly.

The beggar began to understand and enjoy Jasper Bartholomew's discomfort. It was a rare treat to see his cat look guilty and bothered with his own behavior.

"Well," said the beggar, adding kindling to Olivia's fire. "Answer the question Jasper B. Do you expect her to do all the work all the time?"

Jasper glared at his master but said softly to Olivia, "I'm sorry."

The beggar began to enjoy himself even more, for he had suffered a great deal of inconsideration from Jasper's own sauciness and independence. But now, he saw his cat as just a pushover whose will of iron had become a little twig!

"I think it's time to go home. We can leave right after breakfast," suggested the beggar to Jasper, knowing trouble was going to erupt.

"I think I'll stay here," said Jasper softly without looking at his master.

POW!

Jasper received a blow that knocked him rolling over and over.

"I should think you will!" informed Olivia, ready to give Jasper another clout for not being more forceful with his answer. "I should think you definitely will!"

The beggar burst out laughing and couldn't stop. His insolent, snobbish cat, who was used to giving ultimatums, was now reduced to—

"Who's there, please?" called out a gentle, melodious voice.

Shocked, the beggar turned.

It was Princess Gwyn-o-cheri.

At the sight of her, the beggar felt the same lightning shock. The same electrical charge that dashed and galloped through his muscles, nerves, and brain. The same feeling to rip open his mouth.

"Close your mouth," ordered Jasper. "You look disgustingly stupid with it open so wide."

The beggar tried to close his mouth, but the electrical force was too great for a mere human to oppose. Jasper leapt up on the beggar's shoulders and nudged the jaw, closing it with his paw.

"You are rather an embarrassment to me with your tonsils showing, you know. Besides, you show terrible, bad manners."

Jasper remained perched upon his master's right shoulder, one paw extended, snapping the jaw shut over and over. The electricity just kept spinning down and around, causing the beggar's mouth to open again and again.

13

The beggar tried to speak but nothing would come out.

"What are you doing in my bedroom?" frowned the princess. "This is most unappreciated."

"Say something, oh laughing master!" said his cat. "Just a moment ago, you were such a delightful comic. And now, you have a serious speech impediment."

"Ugh," gulped the beggar. "Ughmostomos . . . dphomlomma."

"You are not making any sense, Sergeant. Why . . . you're not the castle sergeant! Who are you?" Princess Gwyn-o-cheri peered closer. "Why, you're the stranger! Weren't you placed in the dungeon to be *TWITTLED OR TWADDLED?*"

As the princess spoke, she looked into the beggar's eyes, and as she did so, the same strange disaster began to take hold of both her knees. A numbness and weakness, which now was of frightening proportions, caused her to wonder if she could remain standing very long in the presence of the beggar.

"An absolute disgrace is what this is," she thought. "Every time I am near this . . . man, my legs become jelly, my heart begins to pound heavily, and my breathing becomes patchy. Is this perhaps some sort of horrible allergy or is my liver giving me the elbow?"

Before she could adjust her thoughts and deduct any meaning from them, Na-Nicky the Huntsman appeared, having just overheard what the princess had said.

"The term used by Lord Raisinkatz," Na-Nicky correcting her clearly and calmly, "is *ZIGGLED AND TWIGGLED*, your Highness. He would become most unhappy with you to hear you mix up the wording of his favorite punishment. It goes without saying that it is all right if he does so, but others are not allowed this privilege."

"Well, *Z-Z-Z-ZITTLED AND TWIDDLED*—whatever. I wouldn't have allowed it to happen to him. I mean . . ." The princess became flustered and her face blushed a pretty pink. She took care to look away.

The beggar, finally able to move his once nerveless

jaw, tried a smile, was unsuccessful, tried to brush his cat away, was unsuccessful with that too, but finally blurted out in desperation.

"Princess Gwyn-o-cheri, I came here to find my lost cat and gosh, you're terribly beautiful and my cat keeps

getting mad at me because he insists on treats of dried fish chips all the time and you're the most beautiful girl I have ever seen in my whole life and when he doesn't get them he runs. You're not really going to marry whoever your uncle picks out, are you?"

"What's this about running away because you don't get treats all the time, Jasper?" demanded Olivia.

"That's in the past, my dear. The past is the past. Best forgotten. Foolish bachelor-type thinking. Not sensible at all," Jasper hastily pointed out.

"I should certainly hope it is all in the past!"

Olivia proudly smiled at the little kittens as she spoke, but changed her expression to that of a dangerous mien when she looked back at Jasper.

"He was actually taking advantage of every opportunity," inserted the beggar who recovered his speech by not looking at the princess. "As he himself admits, foolish bachelor-type thinking, you know. He used to say things like lots of other fish in the sea, trees in the forest, flowers in the garden," continued the beggar, knowing full well he was adding fuel to the fire.

"Indeed!" Olivia's words were covered with a frost which had never seen the warmth of the sun.

Princess Gwyn-o-cheri sat up, concerned. "You mean to say it doesn't matter to either of you which fish or what tree or whose flower?" Her brow was furrowed and her words matched the chill of Olivia's single word. Her cold look suddenly had much in common with that of her cat.

"Please, don't fight. You're just getting to know each other," reminded Na-Nicky hopefully.

"No, no, no!" was the beggar's answer to the princess' question. He saw that he had made a serious mistake. "I was just explaining Jasper's personality to Olivia. You see Jasper Bartholomew is not the easiest cat to be master of—"

"Just the same, your meaning is quite clear." Princess Gwyn-o-cheri was not one bit mollified. Her gentle eyes were now narrowed. Her soft voice was cutting like a saw blade through a tree.

"You're right," offered an agitated Jasper. "That's what he meant, Princess. What's more, he's totally without taste or manners. Haven't you noticed how he drops his mouth open when he looks at you? It's pure disrespect. Observe him right now. His mouth is open, trembling uncontrollably and even drooling. How disgusting."

"I felt sorry for him and assumed it was due to bad tonsils or a weak temporo-mandibular joint," suggested the princess, her voice softening somewhat at the thought of someone's affliction, for she was a very kind person. "Isn't there something wrong?"

"Not at all! It's all just bad manners and poor taste. Or the other way around, poor taste and bad manners," smartly replied Jasper, regaining composure, feeling better and better about getting even.

Na-Nicky groaned in his usual clear and calm manner. "Please don't fight. I have such great hopes that you two would like each other."

Olivia flared up and raised her paws. "Jasper, it's certainly not your place to put down your own master. Shame on you! Your own manners are not that exceptional, especially now that you have certain responsibilities which you gladly appear to be shirking.

Make up by saying something complimentary about your master right now."

14

Jasper looked at Olivia's raised paw and wisely decided to abandon the ship which sailed with the cargo of his earlier thoughts.

"He is a good master. Not too bright. Physically clumsy and inept from a cat's point of view. But he possesses an above-ordinary intelligence for a mere human. Well . . . I guess . . . he does . . . try." The last sentence Jasper said with long drawn out reluctance.

Olivia lowered her paw slowly and cautiously, not quite sure of his sincerity.

As proof of good fellowship, Jasper leapt up on the beggar's shoulder and licked his face.

"Does this mean we're friends again?" asked the beggar hopefully.

"Don't push your luck," murmured Jasper softly, now licking his paw. "I was forced into this, you know."

"Please, don't fight," said Na-Nicky the Huntsman, whose hearing was all too good. He kept rubbing his hands nervously, looking from the princess to the beggar, to Jasper and Olivia, then back to the princess.

The princess remembered something. "What did you say about my being beautiful and whether I should marry or not marry someone who my uncle picks out?" She was addressing the beggar. "You were there when my uncle made me of marriageable age, weren't you?"

"My tongue-tied, open-jawed master would like

to marry you, so we can all live happily ever after together," proposed Jasper.

"I would lob us like us kind marry live toggather happy happy . . ." slobbered the beggar. The electrical circuit in his brain jammed and he was again trying to speak with his mouth open. He couldn't speak any more. Jasper had to race up and push the beggar's mouth shut.

"Please accept his proposal of marriage," requested Jasper.

"Yesh, pleeze akept," repeated the beggar, slurring his words.

"Please, please accept," added Na-Nicky hopefully in his clear and calm manner. "He's really a very nice person. Comes from a good, steady family with proven chromosomes."

"My goodness! I don't know if I want someone who needs his cat to speak for him. What kind of relationship would that be? And what of chromosomes? Am I to understand that you are considering me for breeding stock? What kind of relationship are you intending?"

Olivia, who had half-listened until this time, having busied herself with her kittens, satisfied that the most timid one had enough to eat, spoke up. "A very good relationship, your Highness. He appears of good size and proportion with only minimal detracting features such as the jaw problem. But Jasper will assist him and make him

reasonably presentable. Yes, I think it will work out very well."

"Now, I have my cat, as well as an uncle, telling me what to do. I don't know if I like this," pouted the princess. "I think—"

15

"WHAT'S GOING ON HERE?"

It was Lord Raisinkatz, shouting as usual as he entered.

"SERGEANT, WHY HASN'T THE BEGGAR BEEN BROUGHT DOWN FROM THE DUNGEON TO BE *ZIGGLED AND TWIGGLED?*"

"Right away, Lord Raisinkatz!" saluted the beggar, turning away so his face was hidden. He briskly left the room.

Jasper followed. But first, he leapt in front of Lord Raisinkatz and gave himself a good shake, setting loose all manner of hair, carpet dust, and whatnot.

ACHOO!

The lord's sneezing had begun.

ACHOO! ACHOO! "I PERMITTED ONE CAT BUT NOT THIS MANY!"

ACHOO! ACHOO! ACHOO! "GUARDS, GET RID OF THESE FESTERING FUR-BEARING FELINES IMMEDIATELY!"

Three guards rushed in, but froze in their steps. Olivia was standing up on her hind legs and threatened them, her claws in readiness.

The princess warned, “I don’t think it wise to go near a mother cat. Trying to take away her children is not a good idea. Indeed, you may suffer a lot of pain and discomfort for trying.”

“She speaks the truth,” advised the huntsman clearly and calmly.

“GUARDS, DON’T LISTEN TO THEM. OBEY MY COMMANDS!” ordered Lord Raisinkatz.

“We’re obeying, my lord,” whispered the first guard moving forward.

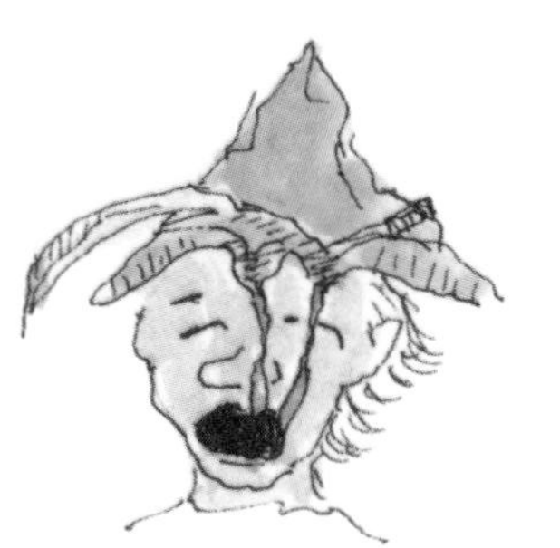

“Ouch! Ouch!”

“OW!” shouted another loudly.

Olivia moved quickly from one guard to the other and scratched just enough to let them know that this was only a preliminary action, minimal and gentle, compared to what was to follow if they persisted.

“WOW! OW! OW!” shouted another guard also out loud, forgetting the Law of the Land.

“WHAT? HOW DARE YOU! YOU SPOKE ABOVE A WHISPER!” shouted Lord Raisinkatz, his face turning red and purple and green. “YOU BROKE MY LAW!” The colors on his face blended together. “IF YOU ARE ABLE TO BREAK THIS ONE

SO EASILY IN MY PRESENCE, HOW MANY OTHERS HAVE YOU BEEN BREAKING BEHIND MY BACK?"

The lord went out into the hall and called for more guards. When they came in promptly, he pointed at the three who were now bleeding on their faces and hands from Olivia's scratches.

"ARREST THESE LAWBREAKERS! THEY BROKE MY LAW," the lord declared, then he sniffed deeply with great annoyance. As he did so, he inhaled a large dose of cat hair which was flitting about in the air.

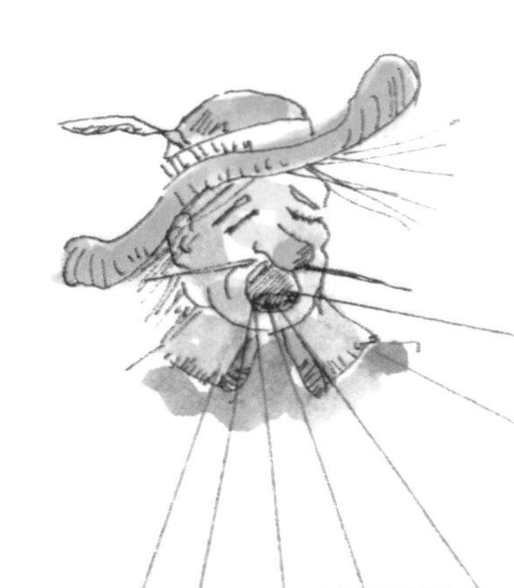

ACHOO! ACHOO! ACHOO!

"THIS IS THE WORST YET. I'M DYING. I KNOW I'M GOING TO DIE! I CAN'T BREATHE! DON'T JUST STAND THERE, PEOPLE. DO SOMETHING!" he rasped.

A guard took great pains to carefully whisper. "Would you like your medicine, my lord?"

"YES, YES, OF COURSE, MEDICINE! SOMEBODY GET MY MEDICINE," gasped Lord Raisinkatz as he doubled over. His allergies were now in full force.

ACHOO! ACHOO!

"It would be wise for you to leave this room," suggested Na-Nicky, wanting to help the lord. "It can only get worse, the longer you remain in a contaminated cat-hair room."

The princess added, "Cat fur travels everywhere. It lands all over everything. You may have to destroy your clothes."

"DESTROY MY CLOTHES?" *ACHOO!*

The thought was too much for Lord Raisinkatz. He loved his silk-woven, tailored garments of reds, blues, and purples, braided with real gold trim and studded with precious jewels.

The lord rushed out of the room. He had forgotten what it was he had commanded. All his guards gladly left with him.

16

Meanwhile, the beggar, Na-Nicky, and Jasper had gone down to the dungeon.

"Are you all right down there?" called the beggar.

The sergeant woke up. His joints creaked and hurt.

"My joints creak and hurt," the sergeant whispered back. "And I don't like it down here. Get me out of here right now."

"Certainly, but only if you become the beggar's sergeant," bargained Na-Nicky. "Turnabout is fair play, you know."

"Yeah, otherwise you'll rot in there and no one will care," shouted down Jasper, sizing up the situation. "Your bones will crack and birds will fly in to eat up the crumbling remains. That is, if the worms and creepy crawly things leave a few tidbits."

"Hush! Jasper. You're saying terrible things," reprimanded the beggar.

"What's more, we might as well get on with it and have them come right now!" continued Jasper in a loud voice. "No use waiting. Peck, peck, peck. That's the way they'll do it. While you're still alive, the worms are feeding."

"Jasper, that's awful! How can you say such things?" whispered the beggar, pushing him back and away from the deep pit.

"It's results that count. Watch," bragged Jasper rather gleefully.

"How can I be your sergeant, beggar?" called up Muster-Buster. "Unlike you, I have been brought up to be a proper person and to eat my dessert last. I'm honest, loyal, and obedient to the orders from my superiors."

"Then if I were your superior, you would obey me?" questioned the beggar for reassurance to his loyalty.

"Yes, but first you would have to be of royalty and that you are not—"

Na-Nicky interrupted. "Only because you saw a beggar's clothes. Right now, everyone thinks he's a sergeant and everyone obeys his orders as a sergeant. If he were to return these clothes to you and wear royal clothes, would you then feel you could obey him?"

The sergeant pondered. None of the soldiers came down here to help him. His lord didn't seem to care who it was that was *ZIGGLED AND TWIGGLED*, so there was certainly no return of loyalty there. On the other hand, if the beggar actually wore the proper clothes and acted like royalty, who was he to question the beggar's right to do so?

"I agree to your terms as outlined, beggar," concluded the sergeant. "In the meantime, could I trouble you for something to eat? Like Shepherd's Pie? I do so like Shepherd's Pie."

"We will return," promised Na-Nicky. And off they went.

17

Jasper went back to Olivia. After receiving information of what had transpired during his absence, Jasper went outside the lord's door and found the royal garments lying there. They were covered with cat hair, carpet dust, and whatnot, waiting to be cleaned.

"Here you are, my almost-competent master," said Jasper, dragging the royal clothes to him.

"Allow me to brush them off first," offered Na-Nicky.

"The lord's clothes? Should I wear them?" asked the beggar.

"Of course," said Na-Nicky, shaking the clothes outside the window and brushing them down carefully. "That does it. Now down to the kitchen for the sergeant's food. Then out to proclaim our royal good fortune to the people."

"But Lord Raisinkatz—"

"Jasper has a way of making sure that Lord Raisinkatz is plenty occupied, keeping busy with his allergies. Sad thing, you know, being allergic to everything, especially to cat hair continually flying in the air."

"You wouldn't, Jasper, would you?"

"Yes, I would," said Jasper. "I would, I would, I would."

"Is that fair play?"

The beggar didn't feel it was quite proper to take advantage of someone who was having health problems.

A sword fight, a horse race, a battle with lances and swords, a man-to-man duel . . . yes. But to take over someone's kingdom this way? It was definitely not an honorable way to win.

"No, it's not fair," agreed Na-Nicky. "But it's a matter of short time that the princess owns everything anyway. You do want to help Princess Gwyn-o-cheri rule the people and end all the edicts that make people whisper and never allow them to know the time or what day it is or what night is, and all that, don't you?"

"I really hadn't thought much beyond getting back my cat until I saw how beautiful the princess is. Don't you think she's the most beautiful person you have ever seen in your whole life?"

The very thought caused the beggar's jaw to quiver and teeter on the verge of dropping open.

Jasper sat down glumly. "Well, I always said you weren't very brainy and that statement proves my entire case. It's quite obvious to anyone that she isn't half as pretty and brainy as Olivia."

The beggar shook his head as though to improve his thinking. (He was really trying to shake his jaw shut.) But when he spotted the lord's fancy clothes lying there to be worn, his jaw relaxed. The beggar then put the royal garments on and set out to feed the sergeant.

18

Having been pulled out of the dungeon and eaten his favorite meal, Shepherd's Pie, the sergeant was in a very good humor. He went around to his guards and explained the change in command.

"You mean we don't have to whisper?" whispered a guard.

"You mean we are allowed to know what time of day it is?" asked another.

"You mean we can now have summer, fall, winter, and spring just like everyone else?" queried a third.

"You mean we don't have to give back half our pay?" asked a fourth.

"Yes, yes, yes, yes. You all make me sick with all your questions. On with your duties!" ordered the sergeant forcefully.

Na-Nicky and Jasper nodded with approval.

When Princess Gwyn-o-cheri spied the beggar in the handsome royal clothes, she experienced the worst weakness in her knees ever, so much so, that this time she almost really fell down.

She told herself this was fast becoming such a serious problem that she needed to solve it posthaste. Having previously discussed this ailment thoroughly with Olivia, they were both of the mind that it was either early arthritis setting in or something worse but equally incurable, namely, love.

The beggar's problem was interpreted less sympathetically by Jasper who, out of pure orneriness, insisted on the diagnosis of *explosive tonsillitis*, caused by a severe strep infection. Or it could be *slack-jaw malfunction* (another diagnosis Jasper made up) insisting that it was a nervous condition of humans, which only improved with time spent on warm sandy beaches that offered soft breezes.

The beggar rejected the two ideas, mostly because Jasper enjoyed telling them to him with too much relish. He realized that the situation only arose when he saw the princess and became worse when he looked into her blue-gray eyes. He rightly concluded it had to do with love—certainly a serious disease, but at least not something little children and wild animals ran away from.

Na-Nicky offered to be their prime minister, serving with an insistent Jasper, who also wanted some important title. They jointly announced a change in the castle command, telling everyone they would have an immediate festival and a continuous celebration for two weeks. Longer, if the townspeople were up to it. They also repealed all the previous laws about such things as whispering, weather, time, seasons, and, of course, taxes.

Everyone cheered and wished them well. Except, of course, Innkeeper Pinchdoodle, who was always known to hold a grudge because he wasn't paid for tattling on the beggar in the first place.

19

Jasper made a daily visit to Lord Raisinkatz, who was dreadfully ill in bed with sneezing, a runny nose, and skin rashes, both imagined and real. The air seemed ever-persistent in carrying cat hair, floating together with household dust, mold, and pollen. Changing from room to room did nothing to help, for the problem seemed to follow the lord everywhere he went.

Once, when Lord Raisinkatz forced himself to walk through the castle, he found not only was he ignored but his loud threats and screams were only smiled at. In fact, when he shouted, he was outshouted right back! He realized for the first time that there is nothing more discouraging or humiliating than being smiled at when you are in a rage. So he sadly went back to his room and didn't come back out. He requested only the services of wise doctors to cure his allergies.

The first doctor to arrive said his allergies were all in his nose, with the air it was breathing. The lord should only breathe through his mouth.

The second doctor found fault in the lord's leaky lungs.

The third doctor treated his sensitive skin and diagnosed that the lord didn't take enough baths.

The fourth doctor agreed that his skin was abnormally sensitive. But he insisted the lord took too many baths.

The fifth doctor was absolutely sure the fault was in the lord's food.

One day, all five doctors accidentally happened to meet at the same time outside the lord's bedroom.

They began to fight so bitterly about the true nature of Lord Raisinkatz's allergies that sixteen guards had to be called to separate the wise doctors who were never allowed in the castle again.

20

Princess Gwyn-o-cheri became queen by default since Lord Raisinkatz simply quit thinking about anything, except his health and any gossip. He did so like gossip and enjoyed talking with his spies about everyone, everywhere, and everything, no matter how badly he felt.

When Na-Nicky wasn't clearly and calmly helping as prime minister, he happily worked the royal forest as a huntsman.

Jasper Bartholomew handled himself very well, being guided with Olivia's firm hand . . . er . . . paw. Every day he went out to the fields, rolled in the pollen, and went to Lord Raisinkatz's room for a good shake.

The kittens grew up beautiful and handsome, but rather strong-minded. All were a delight and were respected for their cleverness. They were welcomed wherever they went in the entire realm. Some took after Jasper and treated humans with mere tolerant disdain. Others took after Olivia and treated everyone with an elegant haughtiness.

The beggar helped the queen rule and, of course, they

married. As time went on, the weakness in her knees improved in that it only occurred eight times a day and then only when the beggar, now king, looked at her and smiled. All in all, they made a very handsome couple and continued to be very much in love as when they first met.

As for the new king's jaw problem, his jaw continued to operate unpredictably, although only in the presence of Queen Gwyn-o-cheri. It was due to Jasper's quick reflexes and rescues that kept the king's jaw from being locked open permanently.

21

Their nearest neighbor, Lord Jinglebee, who had always coveted Lord Raisinkatz's land, was a very forgetful person. He was so forgetful that he often had to ask if he had eaten breakfast or lunch or dinner. Had he taken his bath? Had he gone hunting or fishing earlier that day?

His chief knight Pickory-X liked this about his lord because Jinglebee had to ask if he had paid the knights that month. "By the way, Pickory ole boy, did everyone get paid?"

Pickory-X was honest about a lot of things, but he took advantage of his lord's affliction and always replied, "Whatever your lordship desires."

This answer left Lord Jinglebee confused, which is what Pickory-X wanted, so Jinglebee ended up paying his men again, twice for the same month.

Lord Jinglebee loved to hunt and fish, but he felt that hunting and fishing were much better on his neighbor's land. It wasn't true, but Jinglebee was very easily tricked into thinking so by Pickory-X who loved continual confusion. Each time that they went out and got an extra-big pheasant or extra-huge partridge or extra-large fish, Pickory-X would say, "You realize, my lord, that we are on Raisinkatz's land right now."

After a while, Lord Jinglebee wanted to own this property. And in those days, it was easier to steal land than to complicate things with signed papers.

So, one night they made themselves busy moving fences to have more of the flowing river in their section. But when the Beggar-King and Na-Nicky rode by, they could easily see what was happening.

Running, Lord Jinglebee huffed and puffed when he knew he was caught red-handed. Expecting a fight, he had his knights ride up to meet the enemy.

But the Beggar-King simply asked, "Why is that giant emu so angry at you guys?"

Everyone turned to look and saw a very large emu leaping right at the men, its sharp beak acting like a deadly spear. One man after the other ran from the fencing job as fast as he could.

Astonished, Lord Jinglebee could only stutter, horrified because the giant emu turned on him. "Each m-m-man for him-him-himself!" he shouted and spurred his horse back to his castle.

Pickory-X tried to be brave and move away slower. After all, he was a knight, wasn't he? Bold, brave, courageous, and loyal. But his horse had other ideas.

One look at the charging emu and his horse panicked, galloping away so fast that he sped past Lord Jinglebee and never could be stopped until safely reaching its stall in the castle.

Na-Nicky smiled at the Beggar-King. "It looks as though they've never seen an emu before. Strange that! It's my job to know every kind of animal and fish on this land, but I've never glimpsed such an object like that either."

The Beggar-King, happy with how the kingdom was defended, smiled back, "It'll be awhile before they think about changing fence boundaries again."

22

Correct protocol dictated it was time to invite all the neighboring kings and queens, dukes and duchesses, lords and ladies to a feast that cel-

ebrated the marriage of Princess Gwyn-o-cheri to the Beggar-King. When Lord Jingle-bee arrived, he saw emus in the form of stuffed dolls everywhere.

Even the centerpiece at the large table, where he ate, had a large emu. It looked so real that Lord Jinglebee swore he saw it move. He tried to look away, but it seemed to stare right at him.

"Eyes and neck like a snake," muttered the lord to himself.

His wife heard him and since he was trying to look away from the emu and was staring at his wife, she became angry and slapped him.

"How dare you insult me!" she raged. "My father always told me you would be thoughtless and abusive."

After Lady Jinglebee stormed out of the feast to go home, Lord Jinglebee started to follow when he met Na-Nicky the Huntsman. "I say, strange ugly birds you have around here. Are there many?"

"Emus. New breeding program we have," said

Na-Nicky. "Lays bigger eggs than chickens, ducks, or geese. Mean as all get-out. Be glad to share some live birds with you if you like."

"No, no," shuddered Lord Jinglebee. "No, no."

And he went home, determined never to have anything to do with his neighbor's kingdom again.

23

The Supreme King of All the Kingdoms, King Dinwiddley, ruled over all the other kings and queens, dukes and duchesses, lords and ladies in the entire realm, which included the Raisinkatz kingdom.

At least once a year (more often when he found it necessary) King Dinwiddley would send out his tax collector to gather money. This tax money would finance anything from new jewelry for the Supreme Queen to sending his knights into foreign countries to condemn and annex land for his realm. The Supreme King especially enjoyed annexing land because he would immediately receive taxes from that new property as well.

King Dinwiddley appointed a very conscientious tax collector who was as honest as he could be. His name was Tickory Tettle.

Even though he was honest, Tickory knew he didn't make much of a first impression on anyone. He had a small, pointed nose; slanting eyes; and, no matter how he tried, his hair never looked like it had ever been cut properly.

Worse yet, his appearance was that of a ball. His head was round, his chest and bottom matched perfectly in roundness, and his short arms and legs were as close to round as they could be.

This was not altogether bad because every time Tickory got off his horse, he would always fall down. Being so round, he would never injure himself since he would roll and roll. After the third or fourth roll, he usually managed to get stopped by a tree or a shrub, and got up unhurt.

Because King Dinwiddley had so many kingdoms in such a widespread area from which to collect taxes, Tickory Tettle the Tax Collector was traveling on his horse all the time and rolling off the horse just as many times. He was most unhappy with this part of his job.

And when Tickory was unhappy, he felt anybody, who possessed any shred of decency, should also be unhappy. Since no one with any shred of decency listened to him (or worse yet, agreed with his opinion) he was reduced to yammering at his horse, at the weather, at the sky, at the rolling hills, and especially at the knights who rode with him.

It all had to do with riding a horse. Tickory hated riding horses because his back crunched with every hoof step they made.

Cr-r-runch-ch! Clippity-clop. Cr-r-runch-ch!

He would look back at the knights who rode with him and all of them looked so comfortable, even happy, riding their horses. Why didn't they hurt like he did? It was not only unfair, it was downright indecent.

From the moment Tickory got on his steed, he could hear the grating of his backbones on each other. It sounded like sand grinding between teeth. The same insults were happening to all his ligaments, tendons, and muscles.

And if Tickory would emphasize anything about his pain while riding a horse, he would grimace, "Oh, my aching joints."

Well then, the same insults were happening to all his joints too. Every joint screamed in protest. Not only did his joints, muscles, tendons, ligaments, and backbones crunch and ache and grind, but Tickory Tettle's head would throb.

With each ride, Tickory would yammer to Sir Harry,

"Why can't civilized people put comfortable chairs on the backs of these beasts as the heathens do?"

The leading knight shook his head in disgust. "Next thing you'll be wanting is to be carried," Sir Harry responded unkindly.

"Yes," Tickory reflected. "Yes, indeed, that would be most pleasant." Then for a moment, he began to enjoy the thought so much that he temporarily forgot all his pain. "Ah, to be carried."

At that, Tickory's round face broke into a smile. It wasn't very often that he would smile because, for a man of his position, it simply wouldn't be appropriate to smile. A tax collector was always dignified and . . . (What was the word that meant "above it all"? *Haughty*, that was it.) . . . haughty. A haughty countenance was helpful when listening to a complaining taxpayer. It told everyone that he had heard everything all before. And that all of what anyone was saying was simply boring, boring, boring.

Tickory's work was more a challenge than just a job. Certainly there were the hardships of riding a horse everywhere and staying at inns that offered hard beds and poor meals, but offsetting these were many fringe benefits. The best of them was that he was an important person to be reckoned with!

In fact, one of the more enjoyable aspects of his work was the fear, hate, and hostility he experienced wherever he went. He had come to expect it, look forward to it after he identified himself, and wallowed in it.

He was pleased to no end that otherwise normal and learned people responded so alike to someone who came to empty their pockets of their hard earnings. From kings and queens down to the lowest of low workers, the name Tickory Tettle meant something. What it meant, didn't matter to Tickory as long as he was recognized as someone important.

All in all, Tickory Tettle the Tax Collector was happy and well-suited to his work.

24

Presently, Tickory was crisscrossing the territory and Lord Raisinkatz was next on his tax collection list.

King Dinwiddley had decided to expand his realm by offering to buy the neighboring Jinglebee Kingdom. The offer was turned down for the rather sensible reason that the king's offer was but a pittance. This meant either a higher purchase offer or it meant war. Either way, it was going to cost King Dinwiddley money and that's where Tickory Tettle came in.

"Find the money, Tickory!" ordered the Supreme King. "Get bags and bags of it from Lord Raisinkatz," he demanded. "And don't come back without enough for my needs . . . or else!"

It was the "or else" that concerned Tickory. So in order to be brave enough, Tickory asked for some of the king's men to accompany him. His request was royally granted.

What reminded King Dinwiddley of Lord Raisinkatz was the recent gift that was given to him. It was a magnificent timepiece that was made in the lord's domain. Instead of thinking to thank Lord Raisinkatz for the gracious gift, the king thought of the taxes that Lord Raisinkatz should be paying. Rarely had the Raisinkatz Kingdom paid its rightful assessment of taxes anyway and if the lord had money to manufacture timepieces like the one the king had received, then certainly Lord Raisinkatz should be paying his rightful dues.

King Dinwiddley ordered Tickory Tettle to be especially hard on the Raisinkatz money vault.

For a long time, Tickory had admired Lord Raisinkatz. In a strange way, Tickory appreciated the good lord and enjoyed his difficult mannerisms since both of them found it vastly amusing to try to outwit each other.

He knew the lord was a shrewd businessman and always got a good share of the money from each business in the Raisinkatz Kingdom. The lord's collections were 100% since anyone suspected of not paying got *ZIPPLED AND TWIPPLED* or something like that . . . on the spot!

Tickory shuddered at the thought. But at the same time, he wondered how he could borrow such a technique for his own deadbeat and slow paying accounts.

Unfortunately, recent rumor had reached Tickory's ears that Lord Raisinkatz was no longer in charge of the castle, that he had been rightfully succeeded by his beautiful niece, Princess Gwyn-o-cheri.

Naturally, as a tax collector, Tickory was suspicious of this news. Lord Raisinkatz pulled too many sneaky tricks and, for as many years as he could remember, got away with paying almost nothing to the Supreme King. The lord was an artist—a tax-escape artist. Was this changeover in command just another ruse that Raisinkatz was using to avoid taxes?

Tickory remembered being outmaneuvered so many times by this lord. But each time, Tickory was so impressed and learned so much that he always accepted the pittance which was offered by Raisinkatz, without telling King Dinwiddley of the failure to collect the right amount. How could he tell the king that matching wits with the devious Lord Raisinkatz was no contest? In spite of conniving and trying every type of immoral, illegal, and sub rosa method, Tickory Tettle lost because Raisinkatz always managed to have perfected a new way to thwart Tickory's tax collection.

Of course, he couldn't tell the king of his constant failure because Tickory would lose his job. So he just added tax money collected from other kingdoms to the few coins he had collected from Lord Raisinkatz.

This time, however, Tickory Tettle felt stronger and more determined than ever, especially with the ten good and sturdy knights-in-armor who were escorting him to the Raisinkatz Kingdom. They were ready to pillage and plunder, if necessary, in the name of the Supreme Crown.

This time Tickory Tettle the Tax Collector would show them all. He just had to return with the right amount of money . . . or else!

25

Little did Tickory know the changes that he was soon to find in Lord Raisinkatz's domain.

People were traveling everywhere without

special permission and they were speaking in normal voices. The four seasons were observed after having been forbidden for so many years. Harvesting crops was done when needed. Taxes were eliminated and, most important of all, *time* was acknowledged.

In fact, the word "time" was regarded with such considerable reverence that the people spoke this word in a whisper! It was the only word that was now whispered throughout the kingdom.

When the ban against keeping track of the seconds, minutes, and hours was lifted by Queen Gwyn-o-cheri, her people were so hungry for keeping track of time that they began buying all types of timepieces. Then, after buying all the timepieces they could get their hands on, they each began making their own. My oh my, it took up a good part of their day just to wind all the timepieces that they had purchased and made!

Fairs and exhibits were organized so they could display all these timepieces. After each showing, families would return to their homes and try to make a more exquisite watch or clock than what they saw of their neighbors.

The competition to produce something better than their neighbor continued, until, after only three years, each family had so many timepieces that they were forced to sell them.

The money for these products offered from the other kingdoms were astounding. Well, upon reflection, it really shouldn't be too surprising because these timepieces were a labor of love and so exquisitely crafted. No time or cost had been spared in creating the very best watches and clocks with the finest parts.

In the past, the townspeople had barely made a living with their products of wheat, barley, corn, grapes, and wood carvings. But now, they were making assorted timepieces that were so profitable that they concentrated on just that. Elegant wood carvings were constructed secondarily to add to the beauty of the precision clockworks.

What had once been destroyed by Lord Raisinkatz had become a growth industry. The existence of time had become the most important export of the Raisinkatz Kingdom. Strangers from far away lands began to visit Queen Gwyn-o-cheri's domain, and soon after their arrival, found themselves buying or placing special orders for these magnificent masterpieces.

26

When Tickory Tettle arrived at the edge of Lord Raisinkatz's land, he found no barriers or soldiers.

The guard stations were occupied by wildlife who were quite comfortable. Tickory counted 22 species of birds, 15 varieties of mammals, and 13 types of lizards.

Since occupation is nine-tenths of ownership, they resented being disturbed.

Tickory was horrified!

Lord Raisinkatz wouldn't permit this type of chaos. It must be Queen Gwyn-o-cheri's doing. To be allowed to enter a kingdom freely, without challenges of any sort, was an intolerable insult.

Tickory Tettle mumbled to himself about such a terrible state of affairs. But he expressed no surprise when he found the drawbridge of the castle down and the entrance open.

Was she mentally incompetent? No walls or fences? Open entrance to the castle? If his own king did this . . . Tickory winced at the thought as he and the king's men rode their horses over the bridge into the castle. A few children who were playing on the grounds directed them.

Soon all one and ten found themselves in the back of the castle, surrounded by beautiful orchards and a central garden filled with flowers. Having been cooped up inside the castle for years with no plants, the queen filled every empty space outside with flowers, shrubs, and trees.

The beauty of the surroundings was surpassed only by the most beautiful maiden whom Tickory had ever seen in his whole existence. She had long, flowing, golden-brown hair, and cheeks of apple. Her movements were smooth and gentle, and her voice softly sounded like a musical flute. So this, then, he concluded, was the legendary Queen Gwyn-o-cheri!

Tickory's back pain seemed to vanish as he looked at

the queen. It was several long moments before he could compose himself, state his business, and demand twice as much in taxes as he expected to receive. Anticipating the ordinary reaction after identifying himself as the tax collector, he prepared himself for the usual rejection and hatred.

But the queen made nothing of who he was and what his request was.

Tickory blinked once again at her radiant beauty which shone from her appearance like the light of a hundred burning candles.

Of course, it was a trick! This had to be Lord Raisinkatz's best trick of all: placing the most beautiful, loveliest, most gracious maiden in charge of the kingdom. Who but a shameless lout would hurt the feelings of such a pure, innocent, fair lady?

Tickory Tettle the Tax Collector sighed, "This isn't going to be easy." All his determination to stop losing to Lord Raisinkatz was quickly sliding downhill. "Drat, I'm about to lose again!"

A tear formed on the edge of Tickory's right eye and rolled down his chubby cheek.

27

"Oh, you poor man," fluttered Queen Gwyn-o-cheri. "You must have ridden miles and miles to get here. Please get down and rest. We'll have something for you to eat right away and some comfortable quarters for your stay."

She spoke to all of King Dinwiddley's men cheerfully

about their difficult ride as she welcomed them to her castle.

Tickory gulped embarrassedly. He kept reminding himself that his job was a sacred trust to his Supreme King. Beautiful maidens or not, he had a job to do.

He rolled down from his horse, stopped in front of a gooseberry bush, got up, and bowed. Summoning his nastiest manner and taking care not to look at her directly so he wouldn't lose his will to proceed, he lamented in a high-pitched voice, "Your Highness, you did not even try to repulse me at the entrance. But I, Tickory Tettle the Tax Collector, am here, with armed guards, to collect taxes of five-hundred gold coins or the equivalent thereof. Due now. Payable immediately. Or we shall be forced to pillage and do more serious stuff like that, seeing as we are experienced."

Queen Gwyn-o-cheri looked at him startled. "Why should we stop you from entering and collecting?"

"Because tax collectors are hated everywhere on earth," Tickory pointed out. "It's a rule. You should have put some guards up at the entrances and prevented me from entering with all kinds of excuses like plague, drought, pestilence, something . . . anything! Then, after we had been turned away for the third or fourth time, we would have arrived with more and more knights-in-armor and then you would still make excuses for things that were beyond your control. Or something like that. There are lots and lots of excuses you can use. Don't you have a treasurer to help you with this sort of thing?"

The way the queen kept looking at him was very disconcerting, so Tickory continued in a half-apologetic way. "It's the way Lord Raisinkatz did it and it's the way everyone else does it."

When the queen did not reply, Tickory felt so awkward. He lamely said, "Lord Raisinkatz was very successful at this."

"Oh." The queen's lips parted in a perfect circle and her eyes twinkled. She called a courier to her side and gave him instructions. The courier left quickly after a glance at the one and ten strangers.

Tickory stepped forward to speak more quietly. "Pardon me, Queen Gwyn-o-cheri, but your advisors should have explained this. They should be reprimanded. Lord Raisinkatz always stalled and found so many excuses from paying his rightful share that finally the king would become so exasperated that he would accept any amount just to get the name Raisinkatz off the books!"

"Well then," Queen Gwyn-o-cheri perked up, "since Lord Raisinkatz is no longer in charge, perhaps we'll do things differently and just pay up."

Tickory was speechless.

The queen continued, "In the meantime, feel free to stay or feel free to leave, as you wish. But for now, please hold these flowers for me. And these. Oh, and these too, please."

The tax collector found himself holding large cuttings of daisies, lilies, gladioli, and roses. The beauty and perfume of both Queen Gwyn-o-cheri and the flowers overpowered him that he thought he was in heaven. Tickory Tettle was drowsy from ecstasy. A rare smile flickered across his face until he looked up and spied the startled, staring face of Sir Harry above him.

28

This would never, never do.

Tickory prided himself on treating everyone with the same discourtesy. When he straightened up too quickly, a sharp pain stabbed him in the back and he shouted louder than normal. "HERE!" Tickory shoved the flowers into the arms of the nearest knight and pleaded, "Queen Gwyn-o-cheri, I don't think you understand. I'm the Supreme King's tax collector—not a flower holder." Even though he had shouted, he noticed that his voice had lost its practiced irritation.

This would never do.

The astonishing beauty of the queen was too distracting—too mind-boggling. No matter, he would pull himself together and perform his duty. Tickory Tettle took a deep breath. Beauty or no, his job requirement was quite specific as to what needed to be done.

This fair maiden had to be a ploy on Lord Raisinkatz's part to confuse and befuddle him. Tickory took another deep breath and almost choked from the sweet fragrance of the flowers, but recited in his practiced high-pitched voice: "Your Highness, once again I must recommend that you treat me in the usual traditional manner. Complain. Gnash your teeth. Object. Try to reduce any amount of taxes that I am obliged to levy on you, by insisting on the lack of funds due to (let me help you again) drought, devastation, famine, pestilence, poverty, and miserable, miserable times. Pick any one or all of the above. Then I'll include a severe reprimand to your financial advisor for free."

"But we're very prosperous and happy," replied the queen, smiling brightly.

"Also, I must insist by the authority of King Dinwiddley that I am—what? What did you say, your Highness? Did you say what I thought you said? Prosperous? You actually admit that you are *wealthy*?"

"Why, yes. We have everything we need and then some if that's what being wealthy is."

Beauty or no, his job requirement was quite specific as to what needed to be done. This had to be the cleverest of clever ploys to confuse the issue.

"Am I to understand," stammered Tickory, "that . . . does it follow therefore . . . you mean you're really going to *pay* your taxes? Right now? On my first request? Just like that?"

"Why, yes. I don't see any reason why not. In fact, here's your money." The queen handed the tax collector a sack of gold coins which her courier had just handed her.

Dumbfounded, Tickory looked inside, selected a coin, and bit it. Genuine! And from the feel of the sack, the count was probably correct.

One of the knights made a noise in his throat, getting ready to speak. But Tickory silenced him with a glare. The tax collector had been taught to become very suspicious whenever tax collection was too easy or when the taxpayer was too accommodating.

"Pardon me, Queen Gwyn-o-cheri, is your husband available? Perhaps he would like to express some input about the collection of this money."

"Actually, this is my property, not his," Queen Gwyn-o-cheri softly asserted. "I make these decisions and he always agrees."

Another knight, less constrained than the first, cleared his throat for recognition.

"You have something to say, Reginald?"

"Suggestion, Sire. Let us stay overnight. Since it's getting late and we already have the tax money, we can leave in the morning just as well."

Tickory paused at the thought. He looked at the knight holding the flowers. He noticed four others who were now carrying corn from the vegetable garden. Some were resting in the shade of the fruit trees and others were laughing with the queen's handmaidens. Several were sampling plums and apricots, enjoying the apples and grapes. Legs of the knights-in-armor were all askew as the king's men comfortably lounged in the wicker chairs underneath the willow trees, loosely holding the reins of their horses. He overheard their talk.

"I've never seen strawberries this large before."

"Do you think I can get some cuttings from that delicious, red apple tree?"

Olivia, who had been biding her time with all this company, leapt up on the saddle of one of the knight's horses and answered, "Of course, you can. You're welcome here. These were all gifts from the townspeople anyway."

"A talking cat!" exclaimed Sir Reginald. "Imagine."

Queen Gwyn-o-cheri smiled. "She's the advisor who Tickory wanted me to reprimand."

"A silly cat as advisor and treasurer?" thought Tickory Tettle.

He took a deep breath and surveyed the scene. Perhaps this queen did have mental problems. He had to learn more about her and her husband. Perhaps Lord Raisinkatz was lurking somewhere, smirking at how Tickory was taken in so easily.

"We'll accept your gracious offer to stay until morning!" Tickory heard himself pronounce. Bowing, he added, "With gratitude, your Highness."

"There's plenty of room. The east wing is the cheeriest," replied Olivia. "Gets the morning sun, you know."

Tickory Tettle remained uncomfortable about collecting taxes without any kind of trouble. Somehow there had to be a problem. If it was reported how easy his job was, then just about anyone could do it. He would be dismissed!

The awful thought of a normal life with no one to sneer at or threaten sent shudders up and down his spine until one landed onto his right big toe and stayed there. It hurt as only something can hurt that foretells the future of what it would be like to be a nobody. Imagine just being a nobody. Tickory shuddered some more, adding to the pain in his big toe.

"Is your husband, the king, available?" he asked the queen. "I'd like to meet him."

Olivia laughed merrily. "The king? Huh, he's just like my Jasper. Lay-abouts who are only interested in hunting, fishing, and riding."

"Why, that's not quite true, Olivia," defended the queen of her husband.

"No, it isn't. He also plays the harmonica, hour after hour." Olivia was not to be denied her astute observations.

"The king does take courses of instruction from a learned scholar," noted Queen Gwyn-o-cheri, proud of her beloved's education. "From a well-known wizard at that."

"More play, play, play," emphasized Olivia. "Has he shown us one single thing that he's learned all these months?"

"When the time comes, I'm sure he will show us some magic," justified Queen Gwyn-o-cheri quite protectively.

By then, they had moved next to the castle and the lads had taken away the travelers' horses, stalling them in the barn.

The knights carried the flowers into the hall of the castle and were placing them wherever Queen Gwyn-o-cheri and Olivia ordered. They seemed self-conscious of their efforts, as if they had never done this before.

"I have never done this before," commented one knight out loud.

A single knight stood to one side and jeered at their work.

Whack!

Before he could realize what happened, Olivia had leapt up with one bound and whacked him across the face. "Shame on you! Laughing at someone trying to make a dreary castle a more pleasant place to live. You're stupid and uncouth. Go sleep in the barn!"

"Yeah, Archibold, go sleep in the barn," echoed his fellow knights, now happily relaxing. "We're trying to make a pleasant place out of a dreary room like Whitey the Cat just said."

Olivia snarled a warning and showed her upper teeth. "My name is Olivia and I suggest you remember that!"

"Yes, of course, Olivia it is," they complied as they surrounded Sir Archibold, sticking twigs and leftover flowers and leaves into every opening of his suit of armor.

29

Although Lord Raisinkatz continued to be ill, he entertained his main pleasure in life of playing with the many, many jewels and coins piled up in a secret treasury of his own. It filled the locked room to a height far above the tallest person in town. But as he continued to pay his spies for gossip, his secret supply of treasures dwindled. The lord thought, however, that to know everything about everyone was well worth it.

He knew, for example, when Queen Gwyn-o-cheri arose in the morning, what she did, what she ate, and when she fell asleep. He received full reports on every word that she uttered. Olivia was also closely watched as was Na-Nicky the Huntsman. He was nothing but a do-gooder.

"I do so hate do-gooders!" Lord Raisinkatz once told Na-Nicky to his face. "Everyone has a reason for doing what he does and it has to be a selfish one. How else does one survive in this wicked, wicked world populated with wicked, wicked people like myself?"

Na-Nicky had laughed and didn't even dignify the question with an answer.

Lord Raisinkatz felt his blood pressure increase rapidly at the thought of that one-sided conversation. His red-tomato face burned into a dark umber.

To relax, he immediately conjured up a vision in which Na-Nicky was slowly, ever so slowly, being *ZIGGLED AND TWIGGLED*. He rejoiced as he saw Na-Nicky disappearing into a dark cloud of extreme pain and agony, begging and begging for mercy. With that, Lord Raisinkatz felt his blood pressure ease, his facial color resume red-tomato, and his good humor return.

He chuckled that he didn't have to fear Jasper and that beggar, who is now king. How Jasper would have been hurt to learn that his comings and goings were not of interest to the lord, unlike the Beggar-King who would have cared less one way or the other.

All of this made Lord Raisinkatz feel better and he began to whistle. Hardly had he whistled a note, when one of his spies popped through the window.

At the very same time that this spy popped through, some pushy fur ball squeezed through the spy's feet, trying to make his own mad dash into the room.

"Make way, you idiot tattletale!" pushed Jasper.

Achoo! Achoo! The spy was sneezing and pointing, "You're covered with something awful, something awfully bad that makes me sneeze."

"Get lost," snubbed Jasper. "Go spy on someone."

"Sneeze? Did you sneeze?" asked Lord Raisinkatz of his spy. "I've never known you to sneeze before."

"Anybody would sneeze around that creep of a cat. He must be covered with every kind of morrible-horrible that I've ever known!"

Jasper only deigned to lift up one upper lip and snarl softly. Then he shook himself but good. He looked over at the spy and added one more shake for good measure.

All manner of dirty-dirt, strawy-straw, dusty-dust, cobwebby-cobweb, grassy-grass, furry-fur, and any other morrible-horrible flew across the room with the strong breeze from the opened window. All of it went right into the face of Lord Raisinkatz.

ACHOO! ACHOO! ACHOO! Lord Raisinkatz screamed. He ran for his medicine while Jasper slipped out the window. The black cat left as quickly as he had come.

"I think you're being put upon, your lordship," said the spy.

"I do hate cats. I hate them so much," groaned Lord Raisinkatz between sneezes and coughs. "In fact, I extend my hatred to all flowers, birds, and animals. The feeling must be mutual, I say, for whenever I look at a flower, it *wilts*; when I spot a bird, it flies away *squawking*; and when I see an animal, it *runs* as though it fears for its life."

"Probably none of them are really worth getting to know, your lordship."

"Not worth knowing? What an original thought! I like that. Indeed I do. That is an Eternal Truth. Indeed, I must remember that: Not worth knowing. Remind me to reward you for that."

The lord wanted to whistle again, but his spy spoke before a note was whistled. "My lord, I need to report to you that Tickory Tettle the Tax Collector is here."

Shocked by the news, Lord Raisinkatz whirled around on his heels. He had a litany of questions to ask:

"Tickory Tettle is here?
How did he get in?
Wasn't there any warning to lock the gates?
No guards posted?
No one lifted the drawbridge?
The castle doors weren't barred?
No messengers were sent to say we
were gone on an extended vacation?"

"Quite the opposite, your lordship. There are no guards in the guardhouses anymore and the gates are permanently open. Remember, people can come and go as they please. I told you about this before."

"Yes, it was such a fantasy of fumbling foolishness that I just couldn't believe you. My brilliant mind can't comprehend such utter insanity-in-an-ity. But my people did give Tickory the usual excuses and turned him away?"

"No, my lord. That girl, Gwyn-o-cheri, not only allowed him in, but welcomed him and the ten knights who came with him. She even paid the taxes on the spot! What's more, she offered them a place to stay the night and didn't mention any payment. You should have seen the knights helping decorate the castle with flowers and such." The spy chortled.

"Devious girl! She's going to trick them somehow." Lord Raisinkatz leapt up and laughed with delight. "She was watching and learning after all. Ha, I can't wait to hear how she does it. You must report everything."

"Sorry, your lordship." The spy shifted his weight uncomfortably and looked at the tile floor.

"Sorry? Sorry for what? Is it possible . . . is it remotely possible that such is not the sequence of events which I just outlined?"

"Yes, your lordship. It would appear she is going to do exactly what she says."

"Pay the taxes? Not trick them into giving it back? Has she lost every single drop of her inherited blood? Has she none of the true character that her ancestors struggled to leave her?"

The spy was familiar with Lord Raisinkatz's rage and its dire consequences. It was time to leave.

"I'll be going now, your lordship. I may be missed."

"Hmmm, well, keep me informed. To think my niece has lost all the cunning and treachery that our family has carefully nurtured over so many centuries."

"Lord, one more thing. May I suggest you keep the windows locked against that sneaky cat."

ACHOO! Raisinkatz couldn't help but sneeze. "Just the thought causes me to suffer. But I have placed my calculating brain into action and have created a plan to get rid of that cat. Yes, a plan that will work perfectly to get rid of him and all my enemies . . . forever! Tell my other spies to come quickly. Now away with you."

Lord Raisinkatz rubbed his hands together. The thought of seizing and capturing Jasper made him glow all over. The warm feeling of happiness which swept throughout his entire body increased the flow of vital juices to such an extent that Lord Raisinkatz rocked back and forth, and broke into song—a song which he sang softly to himself with the greatest of pleasure:

"Forgive your enemies—rot!
Love your enemies—what rot!
Instead, I prefer that bygones be bygones
since enemies I have none.
Using a tad of cunning and a tincture of grace:
I'VE DISPOSED OF THEM ALL!"

30

Northwest of the largest forest in the Raisinkatz Kingdom was a wide flowing stream that was well-known for its rainbow trout. The Beggar-King and the huntsman were fond of this place.

But unfondly, Na-Nicky rubbed his left shoulder. "Something isn't quite right," he said.

"We need more fish," responded the Beggar-King.

"Something else," added Na-Nicky. "Something very important."

"We need more game for the table," the Beggar-King suggested.

Na-Nicky shook his head.

The king looked puzzled. "Perhaps a larger party is coming than we allowed for?"

"More serious than that. I have a feeling Tickory Tettle is going to cause trouble," worried Na-Nicky.

"Nothing Queen Gwyn-o-cheri can't handle. Besides, she has Olivia to back her up." The Beggar-King knew the strength of these females.

"Whatever it is, I think we should be heading back," suggested Na-Nicky. "My bones are aching and when the pain jolts the left fibula as well, then it's a serious situation."

The Beggar-King shrugged and packed his gear. Na-Nicky had been right all too often, so they started back towards the castle. It was a full day's journey to get there.

Jasper ran up to them before they had traveled more than two and twenty-thousand hectometers.

"Lord Raisinkatz is on to me," he gasped.

"On to you regarding what?" wondered the men.

"The allergy stuff. You know, my daily roll and shake. He has now made the connection. But it took the help of a spy." Jasper was distraught.

“So what will happen?” The Beggar-King seemed unperturbed.

“If there is no cat agitating his allergies, Raisinkatz will no longer stay in his room. Instead, he’ll be able to make visitations to distant parts. Perhaps to loyal friends who may be willing to help him return to power.” Na-Nicky rubbed his joints some more. “Remember, Lord Raisinkatz has quite an accumulation of jewels and coins hidden in his secret treasury. Purchasing friendship is not an unheard thing these days.”

“Well then, can’t we just purchase it right back?” shrugged the Beggar-King.

Jasper winced at his master’s simplicity. “Easier said than done, profound-thinking master. Some people, who are bought, have the gall to stay bought!”

“Let’s hurry back.” Na-Nicky increased his pace and his mouth formed a grim line as he held his painfully tender radius and fibula.

31

"Psst, Tickory!"

"I'm in bed. Let it wait till morning."

"Psst, over here. Come, I want to talk to you."

"Who's there?"

"A friend, a like-minded comrade, if you will, who has nothing but your best interest at heart."

"Why, Lord Raisinkatz!"

"Hush! I must talk to you in secret."

Tickory Tettle's brain went into high gear. Finally, this was more like it. Intrigue, plots, secret confabs, offers and counteroffers, compromises. He squirmed at the pleasure of trying to guess Lord Raisinkatz's scheme. It was always such fun.

Settling his agitated thoughts, Tickory pompously recited, "I am authorized to listen to whatever may benefit the Supreme Crown."

"But, Tickory, look at these sapphires and diamonds. They can be yours for a mere favor."

Tickory Tettle gasped at the luster of the jewels which Lord Raisinkatz held out to him in his hand. Then he remembered with whom he was dealing. "Bribing an official emissary of King Dinwiddley is a punishable offense."

"Come off it, Tickory. This has nothing to do with your tax collections, which I'm given to understand, is already in your possession."

It was true. He had the money well guarded and distributed among three trusted knights for safety. Suspicion welled in Tickory's ample chest which jiggled like curdled cream as he turned to watch Lord Raisinkatz's face. "Seems to me I've never won with you, Lord R. You have managed to outwit and outsmart me at every turn. Dealing with you has been one learning experience after another. Why would it be any different this time?"

"Because you would have all these precious jewels in your hand before performing the favor, that's why," rasped Lord Raisinkatz.

Tickory Tettle looked at the shining jewels which beckoned him and he couldn't help reaching out to touch them. Lord Raisinkatz gleefully watched Tickory's gestures and quickly poured them into his outstretched hand. He knew his man.

"What type of favor?" Tickory's eyes narrowed at the thought of the dire punishment meted out to a tax collector who faltered in his duty and failed to properly remit all the money to the royal treasury.

"A favor of simply letting me ride with you to a few of the neighboring castles. At most, it would be only a few hundred cubits out of your way."

"Would you be alone?" Tickory suspected treachery.

"I, myself, alone," Lord Raisinkatz assured him softly. "No one else. But we must start before dawn while it is still dark."

"These jewels you offer me just to let you ride with us. Nothing else?" Tickory smelled a rat. "Lord Raisinkatz, how gullible do you think I am? You could have ridden with us without payment."

"Well, all right, I did want you to simply, and it is simply with no effort on your part, merely remain visible while I have a short, very short conversation with the lords of the castles." In his conniving, convincing way, Raisinkatz reminded Tickory, "So-o-o little effort for so-o-o much payment."

"What else, Lord Raisinkatz?" Tickory wondered.

"Nothing else, I assure you. Merely wait for me. Here are the jewels." Raisinkatz placed them carefully into Tickory's fat little hand. "Why not try to trust me?"

"Trust you?" Tickory pocketed the jewels quickly.

"Lord Raisinkatz, did you hear what you just said?" He laughed so merrily that his belly shook. "Trust you, ha-ha."

Lord Raisinkatz's eyebrows arched and his teeth showed to the gums. "Blasphemy, you're right! Those are terrible, inappropriate words for me to use. Listen, Tickory, tell no one I said, 'Trust me,' or my reputation will suffer mightily."

In agreement, the tax collector's head shook, shaking along with his jolly belly.

Then the lord spun around and around in happiness, for he knew Tickory Tettle would be of enormous help to him.

32

"Gone?"

"Yes," nodded Queen Gwyn-o-cheri, "everything was quite pleasant. They even took some seeds and seedlings to plant around King Dinwiddley's castle."

Na-Nicky knew something was not right. "Something is not right," he wisely said. "My radius still aches and my fibula still hurts."

"Fah!" Olivia remarked. "Lord Raisinkatz is our only problem and Jasper has taken care of that."

Jasper became suddenly busy examining something outside the window.

"Jasper!" called Olivia. "You have been visiting the lord every day, have you not?"

“That I have,” said Jasper still looking out the window.

Olivia knew her man well and realized something in his answer was not right. Slowly walking over to him in a pouncing manner, she asked, “What did you do wrong?”

“Made the mistake of going there at the same time his spy was reporting in,” confessed Jasper.

“Which spy?” asked Na-Nicky. “I know them all. Rather a dim lot, I must say.”

“Blathernose.”

“Ah, yes.” Na-Nicky remembered him well. “He’s the brightest of the dimmest.”

“What happened?” Olivia cuffed Jasper. “Why do we have to knock information out of you? What happened?”

Jasper ducked a second blow and voiced, “As I slipped between the spy’s legs, I caused Blathernose to sneeze. He then suggested to Lord Raisinkatz that I was carrying dirty-dirt and all that, and anyone would sneeze and have allergies to all that stuff. It was true. I picked the worst stuff I could find. Even started an allergy on me!” Jasper stood up to show the rash on his belly, begging for sympathy.

Ignoring Jasper’s rash, the Beggar-King asked, “Where is Lord Raisinkatz now?”

“Gone, your Highness,” interjected a servant.

“Gone?”

“He left early this morning before dawn with Tickory Tettle and all the armed knights.”

"I knew something was not right," confirmed Na-Nicky. "My fibula never lies."

"Oh, dash your fibula!" criticized Olivia. "Ride after the lord and see what type of trouble he is stirring up."

"We haven't had breakfast yet," lamented Jasper. "I did run after our king and Na-Nicky to tell them. And we hurried back here, taking the slightest time to sleep or eat."

"But you forgot to tell us Lord Raisinkatz has plans. A small oversight that is going to cost you a breakfast. Off you go. Now, go find him!" Olivia would not be denied.

The three males looked at one another. They had slept in their hunting and fishing clothes all week, and were cold and tired. They looked back at Olivia and realized it was smart not to try her patience when she began angrily waving her paw back and forth.

Queen Gwyn-o-cheri tried to intervene with "Oh, Olivia." But she could see from Olivia's flashing eyes that she would not budge and, all too often, Olivia had been as right in her predictions as Na-Nicky was in consulting his fibula. Queen Gwyn-o-cheri looked pathetically at her husband and his jaw immediately dropped open.

"Saddle our horses!" commanded Na-Nicky to the listening servants.

The Beggar-King went over to Queen Gwyn-o-cheri and kissed her soundly. She giggled as his jaw quivered and tickled her chin. "We must what we must," he tried to say as his jaw continued to quiver and became slack.

But the words came out as "Wo mo wha wo mo."

Jasper looked up at his master. As he jumped up on the Beggar-King's shoulder, he said somewhat discouraged, "Oh, I wish you would learn to close your own jaw by yourself."

33

There had been a strong dew during the night, so it was easy to follow the hoof prints of the horses. Tracking was part of Na-Nicky's ordinary work. But each time he came back from the castles with puzzlement on his face.

"There is puzzlement on my face, you notice," he expressed to the others. "Due to unusual findings. All horses, including the heaviest, waited while a single horse went to the castle and returned."

"That may leave Lord Raisinkatz as the one entering the castle and the heavy tax collector staying with his men," said the Beggar-King. "Let's go ask them what he wanted."

"Why should they tell you?" questioned Jasper. "It'll be easier for me to go and listen to their conversations."

Before they could speak, Jasper had run into one of the castles. About an hour later, a limping Jasper returned.

"They almost caught me!" he cried tiredly. "I had to use my extremely superior cat brain to get away."

"You drew blood," observed the Beggar-King.

"I drew blood indeed. Lots of blood in order to escape and that, my dear king, is good, sufficient reason for this blood. But I did find out that Jinglebee owes Raisinkatz a good deal of money from their gambling. Raisinkatz is trading Jinglebee's debts for big favors."

"You did well, Jasper," praised the Beggar-King. "But I'm sorry you got hurt." He picked his cat up gently, placed him on the saddle, and stroked him, whereupon Jasper purred softly, relaxing from his good efforts.

Hardly had he done so when the castle drawbridge came down. Trumpets sounded and a large group of knights galloped towards them.

"Trouble," said Na-Nicky.

"Trouble," repeated the Beggar-King. "And just last week all the Jinglebees enjoyed a fine dinner with entertainment at our place."

"Yes," said Na-Nicky, "the emus brought a lot of excitement into the lives of the dull Jinglebees."

34

"My League," Lord Raisinkatz bowed to King Dinwiddley. "Against all honorably accepted arrangements, my domain has been confiscated by a young damsel, my niece, who wedded the first whipper-snapper wizard that happened by. He has turned her against me—my own flesh and blood—through the immoral use of callow youth, music, and what passes for charm these days. Against her basic, true wishes, my niece has been forced to abandon me!"

King Dinwiddley looked down at Lord Raisinkatz. As he did so, he cocked an eyebrow to his right where Queen Dinwiddley sat. She looked fast asleep.

"She only pretends to fall asleep when she feels no mercy for the supplicant," he thought. To the left was his advisor. He heard a hiccough.

Hiccup!

Whenever his advisor had a complicated plan, he began to hiccough.

Hiccup!

King Dinwiddley leaned over and waited for the advisor to say something, keeping well out of the way of any wayward sneeze.

"Speak!" he commanded.

Hiccup! The advisor began: "The lord states he has friends to . . ."

Hiccup! "He has friends to help him. Have his friends . . ."

Hiccup! "Have his friends help us first. Then . . ."

Hiccup!

The king was getting impatient. "After which we will judge what to do with his own problem, will we not?" finished the king sagely. But his sageness was a mite loud for the queen who stirred and opened her eyes.

"Jewels," she cooed languidly, stretching out her arms. "Jewels," she repeated. "His type always hides jewels. I'd like to see them."

"The queen states you have hidden jewels, Lord Raisinkatz. Is this true?" questioned the Supreme King.

Lord Raisinkatz trembled. His color changed to a dusky hue. The entire court listened for his answer. He started to speak.

Achoo!

He then sneezed again and again. *Achoo! Achoo!*

Each time he began to speak, a sneeze with fitful coughing began. *Achoo! Cough, cough, cough.*

Tickory Tettle came forward and kneeled. He was holding a satin pillow on which he had placed the jewels given to him by Lord Raisinkatz.

Everyone gasped at the reflected light from the stones.

"Cut glass, your Highness. These were given to me if I would allow him to travel with us. He visited each castle on the way and received pledges from knights to do battle for him. He inferred that this was your wish as well." Tickory made a wan smile in Lord Raisinkatz's direction.

"And he paid you in cut glass, Tickory? How droll,"

the queen laughed. "If he had these, then he has the originals!"

"Perhaps cut glass was all he thought your services were worth," suggested the king with a smile.

Tickory frowned glumly. He didn't like jokes like that. They often led to unemployment.

Lord Raisinkatz finally regained his voice and sputtered, "Swindled! I was swindled. These jewels were given to me in good faith as genuine. I know not . . ."

Achoo! "I knew not . . ." *Cough, cough, cough—*

The king held up his hand. "No one has ever swindled you, Lord Raisinkatz, and lived to tell the tale. I shall order the knights whom you have summoned and will use them for my own neighborhood property improvements. You will be obliged to pay all of them during their temporary service with me. Dismissed."

Lord Raisinkatz bowed deeply and backed out of the king's sight.

35

"Well done, Tickory! You are a good and faithful servant."

"Thank you, my king. May I have leave to request a favor?"

The Supreme King nodded to go ahead.

"Your Highness, my back is out. Could I have assistance in lifting me up to the standing position. The horse, you know."

The king smiled and motioned his guardsmen to lift him up. Tickory grimaced and groaned.

Most embarrassing was the queen's laughter. "Tickory, you are most delightful! You put on one show after another. I can hardly wait for your next court appearance."

Lord Raisinkatz was waiting in a corner. As soon as he saw that they couldn't be heard, the lord grasped Tickory Tettle by the coat lapels. He rasped, "How could you do this to me, Tickory? Have I not taught you trickery, Tickory? Have I not shown you outstanding examples of devious deceptiveness and downright dastardly degenerateness? Is this how you repay me when I am alone and vulnerable?"

Tickory bowed deeply. "Honor me, for I have learned well, Lord Raisinkatz. Now you must find real coins and real jewels to pay the knights. You have only a short time or the king's wrath will be incurred. Hadn't you better return and get the proper payments? Or do you prefer that the king organize a search of your entire castle for whatever secret treasures you have hidden so he can confiscate it all?"

Lord Raisinkatz felt bitter tears flow down his face like warm, rancid olive oil. He licked them and reflected how unfair this all was. Tears were for others, not him. What was the use of holding himself up as a fine example of straight-as-an-arrow undeviating dishonesty?

No one appreciated his efforts. He had come with a simple request and was slandered, ridiculed, challenged, and threatened. Someone was to blame.

What had made Tickory inspect those pieces of colorful cut glass so quickly? It could only be that he, Lord Raisinkatz, was such a good teacher! And did he receive appreciation for his teaching talents? Sadly he shook his head and answered "no" to his own question. It was all going so badly.

What he needed was a good omen. But first he had to get rid of the bad ones surrounding him, like pollen and bugs and furry animals . . . like cats. Yes, cats were very bad omens, especially that black cat Jasper. But the disposal of it was left to his spies. Would they bungle the job? He should have taken care of the matter himself before he left. He better check on that now.

Lord Raisinkatz called for his horse. As soon as it was bridled and saddled, he raced homeward like a man possessed by a hundred demons. His luck had to improve.

36

"Should you so desire, I could try to make us all disappear," said the Beggar-King. "It was last week's lesson, and I haven't practiced as much as I should."

"A wizard apprentice tried that once," said Na-Nicky. "And everyone disappeared all right. They ended up lost in a forest miles away from where they started. Let's see what Jinglebee and his men want first."

"Cover me up and hide me on your saddle," said Jasper drowsily. "They may be a mite unhappy if they learn I belong with you."

"Sounds like you did more damage than you cared to mention," surmised Na-Nicky.

"I did more damage than I care to mention," yawned Jasper as he positioned himself for sleep.

The knights drew up and stopped. The leader, Lord Jinglebee, was thin and lanky with a large pug nose. Riding a small horse, Jinglebee's feet almost dragged on the ground.

"Greetings, Lord Jinglebee," frowned Na-Nicky. He didn't like this lord.

"Have you seen a huge, ugly, black beast pass this way? It fights like a tiger."

"Hunting kitty-cats now, are you?"

"It's a wild, ferocious animal possessed of the devil," uttered Lord Jinglebee excitedly. "We must capture it right away."

"Wouldn't it be better to spread out and search for tracks?"

"This animal is too clever to leave tracks. It's the devil incarnate!"

"I would agree to that, you twit," whispered Jasper from undercover.

"What did you say, my lord?" asked Kikory-Kick, one of Jinglebee's knights.

"Nothing important," voiced the Beggar-King hastily. "I once had a pet who was pretty much in that category. Treated well, only to have it change into a lunatic. Since then, I've learned wild animals are impossible to train."

As he finished, the Beggar-King felt a claw steal out from under the saddlecover and scratch his hand.

"True indeed, this animal is definitely a wild one," emphasized Lord Jinglebee. "By the way, your Highness, nice dinner at your place the other day."

"Nice dinner at your place the other day," mimicked and mocked Jasper in a muffled voice.

Jinglebee turned his horse toward the Beggar-King. "It was at your place, wasn't it?"

"Yes, it was a nice dinner at our place," confirmed the Beggar-King.

"Well, we must be off."

The Jinglebee riders rode out of sight as they stayed close together for protection from the mighty feline.

The Beggar-King moved his cloak covering the saddle bag. "Can't you stop getting into trouble even for a moment, Jasper?"

"Shall I tell you what I learned or do I listen to you jabber?" responded Jasper.

"Tell," answered Na-Nicky.

Jasper got up and began telling what he had discovered. "Lord Raisinkatz has asked these knights to come to his castle to restore law and order, and to throw certain people into the dungeon. He told them his authority has been stolen without rightful cause by a conniving magician who casts spells." The cat turned to his master. "That's you, you sly, calculating, conniving conniver! The magician part—well, he doesn't know how you bumble around in your studies."

Ignoring these last comments, the Beggar-King

wearily asked, "Should we press on?"

"Let's go back. I did a great job," bragged Jasper. "And I can't wait to have Olivia hear about it."

"I agree that we return to the castle," advised Na-Nicky.

So they turned their horses around and headed back to the greatest stone castle on the highest hill. Little did they know that Lord Raisinkatz had already raced back to their castle by a shortcut and was already deep in sinister plots for a return to power.

37

Lord Raisinkatz was furious at his hired men. "But he was nowhere to be found!" exclaimed the Number One Spy.

"We set out all kinds of enticements. We know what he likes. Fish cakes are his favorite," added the Number Two Spy.

"Only the kittens came and we couldn't hurt the children," the Number Three Spy pointed out.

"Why not?" shouted Lord Raisinkatz. "Give me one good reason why not. Aren't they dirty, allergy-forming, fur-bearing creatures too? Dispose of them all! And since you have failed your duty to me, you must pay the consequences. Sergeant, zap these three spies with the awesome and terrible *ZIGGLE AND TWIGGLE*. Zap now!"

But nothing happened.

"Hmm, I forgot. There's no one to do it anymore. What a pity! What a loss! What a terrible shame! I must think of some other punishment." Lord Raisinkatz spun around and around, terribly agitated. He stopped. "I know!" He addressed the spies: "You, my dear slackers, pick your own punishment and perform it on yourself. That's the best way to learn not to disobey." He started to spin again.

"Yes, my lord, if we pick our own punishment, it will make us always remember how we failed far better than if you selected one," added Number One Spy.

"Wonderful, marvelous idea!" blurted out Number Two Spy.

"Only a brilliant mind like yours could have thought of it, my lord," praised Number Three Spy.

"You are perfectly correct!" beamed Lord Raisinkatz, his good humor returning as he slowed down his spinning to a stop. "I should have thought of it before. In fact, I must have thought of it before and merely disremembered to put it into action."

All three spies nodded vigorously. "Of course, that's what happened."

Lord Raisinkatz was pleased. "Now we must get to work. Listen closely, and repeat my orders after me so I know you have them right."

Achoo! Achoo!

"Achoo! Achoo!" repeated the spies.

"No, no, I was sneezing, you fools." But Lord Raisinkatz controlled his temper this time. "Listen, your first job is to get my sergeant to come here immediately."

Achoo! "You understand?"

"Achoo! You understand?" the three spies repeated, nodding to one another.

"Stop repeating everything after me. That irritates me." Raisinkatz waved his hand to scoot them out the door. "Oh go, get outta here. Go get the sergeant now."

The three spies were more than happy to leave.

Lord Raisinkatz turned to the window and looked out. "Here, kitty, kitty. Here, kitty, kitty, kit." He was using his sweetest sounding voice ever, but had no luck. The cats didn't even look up at him. "Blast their gizzards!" he mumbled.

Again in his sweetest tone, he sung, "Here are some nice fish cakes. Delicious fishy cakes. Fresh fishy-wishy cakes. Come, come, little fur-bearers."

Achoo!

But none of the cats would come.

Achoo! Achoo!

Lord Raisinkatz sat in his chair and sulked. No one was cooperating.

When it got to be dusk, there was a knock on the door. "Come in," barked Lord Raisinkatz.

"Begging your pardon," said Sergeant Muster-Buster, "but Spy Number One told me to see you."

"Not 'Spy Number One' but 'Number One Spy,'" corrected Lord Raisinkatz. "There's a difference, you know."

"Regret the mistake," apologized the sergeant politely.

"Good, now listen carefully . . ." Lord Raisinkatz outlined his plan.

"But that would not be fair to Queen Gwyn-o-cheri," protested the sergeant.

"Sergeant, you must obey royalty, must you not?"

"Yes, my lord."

"I am royalty, am I not?"

"Yes, my lord."

"Therefore it follows, does it not, that my wishes are to be obeyed?"

The sergeant looked bewildered.

"Shall I go over it again, Sergeant?"

With no response, Lord Raisinkatz knew the answer, so he spoke very slowly for Muster-Buster to follow. "Sergeant, I am royalty. Royalty and commands from royalty must be obeyed. I command, so you obey. Simple!"

The sergeant shook his head and tried to clear it. He knew something was not right, but he couldn't quite think what it was. Later, he told himself, later he would figure it out.

Lord Raisinkatz stood there waiting. His potato head of tomato-red appeared to be turning slime-green. A very bad sign, the sergeant knew from experience.

"Yes, my lord, I will obey," he concluded hastily.

"Let us not quibble about this again, Sergeant." Lord Raisinkatz spun around. "Now go and perform your assigned duty."

38

"So, the three of you were gone all that time and that's all you found out?" Olivia was in disbelief.

"We thought we did pretty good," defended the Beggar-King of the threesome. "Jasper had a rough time getting away, then Lord Jinglebee and his men were chasing and hunting him down."

"Anyone who can walk while riding a horse can't be much of a threat to anyone," noted Olivia, thinking of Jinglebee dragging his feet when riding his horse.

"What do you think will happen now?" asked Queen Gwyn-o-cheri.

"Oh, the usual," said Olivia matter-of-factly. "Lord Raisinkatz will spy, bribe, and spin around the truth. King Dinwiddley will want more and more money. You know, he's always expanding his territory. He'll demand all of Lord Raisinkatz's treasures in return for helping Raisinkatz back to power."

"We can't do anything, then," sadly Queen Gwyn-o-cheri voiced, in a tone that could still blend with the musical notes of the finest songbirds.

Upon hearing her voice, the Beggar-King felt a smashing jolt of electricity flow through his body and his jaw dropped open.

"Close your mouth," reminded Jasper sharply. "Get control of yourself."

Olivia shook her head. "We'll just wait."

"For him to get control?"

Just then, they heard marching commands. Sergeant Muster-Buster walked in with several guards. They were marching out of step, and their clothes were hanging loosely and fitting poorly. No one had needed soldiers after Lord Raisinkatz lost power.

"Just where do you think you're going?" suspicioned a suspicious Olivia.

"To arrest people on the authority of Lord Raisinkatz."

"And what, per se, are the charges?"

"Misbehaving and willful sedition against the lord," answered the sergeant flatly, avoiding eye contact with Olivia.

"And when you've arrested them, you'll come after us. Is that not true?" questioned Olivia, inching up to make eye contact.

The sergeant looked embarrassed. "Orders are orders. I'm just doing my duty for what I was trained." He stared straight ahead.

"Let me re-train you!" informed Jasper as he sprang up onto the sergeant's shoulder and began to swing his paw. All his sharp claws were extended.

"Stop!" cried Olivia.

Jasper held his paw in mid-air. The sergeant stood straight and like the true soldier that he was, he did not flinch.

Olivia innocently circled round the officer. "Where are you going to keep all these people you are arresting, dear Sergeant Muster-Buster?"

The sergeant's face fell. He blinked his eyes and paused in thought. He knew he should be careful with Olivia. She was terribly clever. But she was right! He had no room for all the people he was told to arrest. Where would he put them all?

"Perhaps I should go back and ask Lord Raisinkatz," he slowly guessed.

"So you want him angry? You know what happens when he gets mad at anyone," reminded Olivia.

Oh, how well the sergeant did know. He shuddered at being *ZZZZIGG* . . . He couldn't bring himself to even think it. "What should I do then?"

"Why, it's obvious, isn't it?" Olivia was setting the sergeant up with her question. "First, you must dig the dungeons," the cat instructed. "And they must be very deep dungeons too." She paused long enough for her advice to sink into the sergeant's brain, then added, "You know how furious Lord Raisinkatz would be if anyone escaped by simply jumping out."

The soldiers groaned at the thought of digging into all those rocks below the castle. "Oh no, not those rocks."

So immediately three of them called out that they were under the doctor's care for severe pains in their arms and legs. Four others asked to be relieved of duty (temporarily, of course) to visit dying relatives. Trying to outfox the others, one soldier asked to be made supervisor of the project because he had degenerative processes of the spinal cord.

"Since when?" quizzed the sergeant of the last soldier. "Since when have you had these degen . . . degenerashuns?"

"Comes and goes," answered the soldier quickly. "I hide the pain well, don't you think?"

The sergeant narrowed his eyes on all of them. Soldiers were one thing he could handle. "Back we go, buckos!" he ordered. "Get shovels and picks, and meet me pronto in the dungeon area. We have work to do."

"What about my doctor's orders?" pleaded one soldier.

"My dying aunt," sobbed another.

"My rotting backbone—"

"Stop!" yelled Sergeant Muster-Buster. "You can take care of all your personal problems after the work is finished. Now march, busters!"

The soldiers moaned and groaned and muttered as they mustered enough energy to march ever so worse than when they came in.

39

Lord Raisinkatz filled two small pouches with jewels and coins, making sure they were all genuine. It would not do for King Dinwiddley to receive false stones a second time. Lord Raisinkatz shuddered at the thought of any dire punishment inflicted upon himself. Punishment was invented for others to bear, not for others to inflict on him.

When he went to get his horse, he heard the clatter of hooves and noises in the courtyard. The knights of King Dinwiddley were led by Tickory Tettle! They rode up to Lord Raisinkatz. "The king needs ten pouches filled with jewels and coins. He asked me to be sure you got the number of pouches correct. So here are the pouches."

"These are enormous pouches, Tickory. The king didn't say—"

"I know, but the queen often changes his mind."

"Blast that woman!" cursed Lord Raisinkatz. "The bloody dickens, she won't be satisfied until I am a poor wretch, unable to feed my large, growing family and powerless to protect the hundreds upon hundreds of people who look to me for spiritual and economic sustenance."

"Is he refusing, I hope?" asked Sir Archibold the Bold, nudging Tickory.

"No, I am not refusing!" swiftly replied Lord Raisinkatz, whirling around on his heels. "Not at all. Not in the slightest. Never! The Supreme King's needs come first and to that end, he may have all the jewels and coins that I possess. Let us all starve and disappear from sight. It doesn't matter."

"Glad to hear it," grinned Tickory. "Now fill up the ten pouches and bring'em here. We'll wait and ride back with you."

"You don't need me. Why not just take the jewels?"

"Oh, we'll just wait for you."

"I promise to follow later." Lord Raisinkatz lifted up the palm of his right hand as a show of honesty. "Lord's honor!"

"We'll wait for you."

Lord Raisinkatz looked at the knights. There were too many and they looked too anxious for battle. Olive oil tears began to flow down his cheeks so he turned away. It wouldn't do for these armored men to see his weakness. He had lived by his wits for so long, only to be outmaneuvered by a simple-minded tax collector. Lord Raisinkatz couldn't give up so easily.

"Won't you wait in the garden and have something to eat?" invited the lord.

"You have just five minutes." Tickory's steely voice indicated that the king's men were not to be trifled with.

Lord Raisinkatz growled, "As you wish." He turned again before they could see the tears stream off the end of his nose and stain his beautiful garments. Olive oil was so oily.

Five minutes later, he strolled down with the pouches.

"There are only nine here," observed Tickory. "And they're only half-filled."

"Blast, I must have miscounted. Not very good at this sort of thing, you know," alibied the lord, shrugging his shoulders.

"Back you go and if they're not completely filled this time, I will come in and fill up the pouches myself," threatened Tickory.

"No, no!" exclaimed Lord Raisinkatz. "My room is privileged, private, and permission is proscribed."

Lord Raisinkatz felt the sharp ends of three lances from the nearest knights. "Tickory told us exactly what you were going to do and you tried to do it. One more chance is all you get," growled Sir Archibold the Bold.

He wondered if these soldiers would understand a gift? Should he try that? He squinted up at them. They were the type who mindlessly obeyed orders. How he hated drudges who could not think for themselves and would not improve their lot in life by accepting a bribe or two! They were in the same category as do-gooders like Na-Nicky.

Sighing deeply, he turned and went back into the castle. Shortly, he came out with the exact amount of treasures that was demanded.

"Let's go!" bullied the first knight, waiting for the lord to mount up.

Slowly Lord Raisinkatz got into his saddle and looked up at the greatest stone castle on the highest hill. Sinister shadows seemed to be everywhere in the crumbling parts of the walls and turrets.

Sadly, he followed the group, reflecting all the time on the few jewels remaining after his donations to the Supreme King, payments to his spies, and his speculations in far-flung businesses.

40

King Dinwiddley's plans for annexing his neighbor's land had run into a snag. The snag continued to be the owner, Lord Jinglebee. When the king tried to explain that annexation was a form of borrowing what he needed, Jinglebee became quite hostile.

This was a most unneighborly reaction because it meant that they had a dispute and disputes had to be settled by battle after battle until someone gave up.

The king was upset. Didn't Jinglebee realize that battles were expensive? There was the borrowing of knights and weapons and the purchasing of food, shelter, clothing, fresh horses, and horse feed to supply the army. It was purchase, purchase, purchase—all outgo and no income.

Worst of all was the increased prices that had to be paid because businesses knew who had to have what supplies. It was no mystery how a sudden "shortage" developed in just those essential items.

The royal treasury was empty. Tickory was against taxing the local people any more. They had been taxed so often and so much that King Dinwiddley's own people started to join in Jinglebee's cause. How disloyal!

Luckily, the king had a lord who had saved a great deal of money over the years. How fortunate he was to have the fine Lord Raisinkatz!

It was too bad, however, that Raisinkatz was so sad. Nothing seemed to cheer him up during the past weeks. Perhaps King Dinwiddley could make it up to him some day.

41

Months later, it was a sorrowful Lord Raisinkatz that was finally allowed to return to his castle.

But once more, he was accompanied by a guard of knights. They were ordered to collect whatever remained of the jewels and money that Lord Raisinkatz possessed.

Lord Raisinkatz slipped off his horse wearily and listlessly, greeted by Sergeant Muster-Buster. The sergeant was ready to report about the new dungeons that had been built in the months that had gone by, but the lord waved the sergeant away. What did it matter now?

"Pardon me, my lord." Lord Raisinkatz looked up wearily. It was Number One Spy calling him from the dark shadows. "Would you like a report?" he whispered.

"No."

"No? Excuse me, my lord. Did you say 'no' as in *no*?"

"Yes, I mean 'no' as in *no*."

"But my lord . . ." Number One Spy couldn't understand this turn of events. Lord Raisinkatz was always so enthused about gossip.

"Go away," advised Lord Raisinkatz.

"Go away?"

"He means scram," interpreted the nearest knight as he jabbed the spy in the chest with a lance.

Number One Spy stood still with his eyes staring at his lord. It wasn't until the second and harder jab hurt enough that moved the Number One Spy to scream, "This is unfair. You need me!"

Lord Raisinkatz hardly heard anything. He handed off the reins to the stable boy and wandered into the castle. Soon he came out with bags and bags of jewels and coins, handing them to the knights.

"This is all of it," he moaned. "Come search for yourselves if you don't believe me."

Saying not a word, the knights took the bags, loaded them on their horses, and rode off. Lord Raisinkatz mournfully watched them disappear with all his money.

"I've saved and scrimped all my life. What for? For nothing. All the fun I could have had spending it! Gone. I'm a ruined man. I'm reduced to nothing. Oh, woe is me. I shall never be happy again."

Even though he knew his olive oil tears would stain his royal clothes terribly, he was so dejected that he let the tears flow wherever they wanted to go. Lord Raisinkatz just didn't care anymore.

42

"Something is wrong with Lord Raisinkatz. He hasn't eaten for two weeks," said the cook to Queen Gwyn-o-cheri.

"How sad. I shall see him right away."

Queen Gwyn-o-cheri went up to Lord Raisinkatz's chambers and knocked on the door. When there was no answer, she opened it and peered into the gloom of the dark room.

"Hello-o-o?" she sang.

She heard a stir in the corner, so she walked in and opened the curtains first. Lord Raisinkatz was sitting in his favorite blue chair, staring into space.

"Why, Uncle, what's the matter?"

"My life's blood is gone. Other than that, nothing is the matter," he whispered.

"What nonsense. You mean your silly jewels and coins, don't you?"

He looked at the queen with sad, solemn eyes. "A Raisinkatz always regards money equal to the blood which flows through his veins."

"Well, if that's all you want, then we'll find some money for you to play with. But what good is all that dead stuff anyway?"

"Don't blaspheme the word, Niece. Money is power and power is money!"

"What good is power if everyone hates you? What good is money if you are sick all the time worrying about keeping it? It's only worthwhile if you do something with it."

"Your ancestors would be appalled to hear those words. You're not talking like a true Raisinkatz. Someone has misinformed you terribly. Who told you that?"

Queen Gwyn-o-cheri paused, somewhat embarrassed. "Olivia told me that."

"It's your stupid fur-bearing cat. And you believe it?"

"*Her*," the queen corrected him. "She's a *her*. She doesn't like being called an *it*."

"*Her* name is Olivia and the queen is quite right," purred Olivia as she strolled into the room. As usual, she made sure she was never too far away from her mistress.

Lord Raisinkatz moaned, "A cat. Always an allergy-producing, talking beastie hanging around."

"Your allergy is gone even with a beastie next to you," Olivia smiled a sly smile. "Haven't you noticed?"

Lord Raisinkatz seemed to awaken as though from a trance. "You're right! I'm not sneezing or coughing. I can breathe without wheezing. And you're standing right next to me!" His eyes lit up, astonished.

"It was all related to hiding your money. Now that your money is gone, your worries are gone," Olivia pointed out.

"You mean . . ." Lord Raisinkatz paused to think.

"Yes," insisted Olivia. "Shall I repeat it?" The cat often became irritated with how slow some human minds functioned. "I notice that some of you humans have a hard time with concepts."

"Then this also means that I can eat what I want, drink what I want, wear what I want, and bathe whenever I want. And no more doctors. I never thought to try that!"

"He catches on quickly. Rather admirable, Queen Gwyn-o-cheri," remarked Olivia tartly. "I'm impressed with his new brain power."

"It's time for dinner, Uncle. Let's go down."

Lord Raisinkatz got up slowly and began to smile for the first time. As they began walking down the hallway, he looked down at Olivia and said, "I owe this insight, this revelation to you."

Olivia was unforgiving as usual. "To me? The beastie you hate?"

"A thousand pardons. I've never met anyone quite like you. As clever as you. Not any talking animal at all."

"How could you? You were always busy counting your money. Now, aren't you sorry you wasted so much of your life needlessly? Think of all the fun you could have had." Olivia's upper lip curled ever so slightly.

"Well, saving money was fun in a way," said Lord Raisinkatz. "I especially miss the counting part. It made me so very happy. Whenever life's sorrows were too hard to bear, counting my money took them away. You know, it's hard to explain one's personal pleasures to another."

"Pure rubbish!" growled Olivia. "It's selfishness that can't be explained, not pleasures."

Then with pleasure, she turned and warmly greeted her many kittens who had just run up to find her.

43

A few months passed and Lord Raisinkatz didn't have to take to his bed with a single illness the entire time. He had so much fresh air at King Dinwiddley's castle that his lungs had been cleaned out. Allergies and such had been long forgotten.

He seemed happier and kept very busy with his "projects" as he called them, leaving on weekends and returning Monday mornings quite happy.

On occasion, a rider would hurry up, speak to Lord Raisinkatz for a brief moment, then leave. Since nothing happened and the lord seemed in good humor, no one thought anything of it.

He plunged with vigor into planting and weeding the gardens. Then one day, as Lord Raisinkatz sat down to rest and think deep thoughts in the beautiful garden with the sun shining down on the gorgeous flowers and blossoming fruit, the clippity-clop of a horse neared. Its shadow crossed over his body. Looking up, he spotted Tickory Tettle.

"Tickory, my friend, hello!" he exclaimed. "Give your back a rest and pull up a chair. Have something to quench your thirst."

Tickory Tettle looked down, puzzled. Was this the sad and depressed lord that he had seen just a few months ago? Or was this another trick?

"Lord Raisinkatz? Is that you?" Tickory was confused.

Lord Raisinkatz threw some dirt into the air, caught some of it, then allowed it to flow through his fingers very slowly. "Why, don't you recognize me in these old gardener's clothes, Tickory? Even lords are allowed to dig in the soil and plant things, just for the pleasure of seeing them grow."

"Yes, indeed, my lord," Tickory agreed with suspicion. "You are quite right, but your line of work seemed to be shouting and ordering and threatening others to do the dirty work."

"Times change. And people change, Tickory," sighed Lord Raisinkatz. "So why are you here, or need I guess but once?"

"The usual," said Tickory glumly. "The battle is going poorly while everything keeps getting more and more expensive. We're gouged on everything. The cost of food and equipment has gone up many fold. They keep telling us there is a shortage of supplies until we pay the increased prices. Then the shortages disappear! We're in a bad way, unless I can find some money."

"So King Dinwiddley sent you out to collect more taxes."

"Uh . . . yes, you can say that," said Tickory more glumly. "But where can I get more money?"

"You've gotten all I have, Tickory. Search the place. You've taken everything I saved for years."

"Many pardons, my lord. It was on the direct orders

of the Supreme King that we empty your treasuries. You have every right to be sad and dejected over it. But may I mention that you look much happier? No coughing and sneezing. No sudden rages." Tickory felt awkward but said it anyway. "Congratulations."

Lord Raisinkatz leaned down and picked up one of Olivia's kittens and scratched its ears. "Did you want to see Queen Gwyn-o-cheri about anything?"

"Well, yes, I need to suggest she make a large contribution to the king."

The kitten snuggled into Lord Raisinkatz's jacket as he laughed and laughed. "Since she taxes no one, she has nothing to offer but the food from her garden and whatever is given to her from the hearts of the people. The last taxes that she paid were all from her own money."

"I was afraid of that," said Tickory most glumly. "Yet the king rages more and more each day as we lose battle after battle. The worse part is the way the prices go up. Merchants are all becoming wealthy—but we can't find who they are. The king will have my head, unless I return with more money." Dejectedly, Tickory turned and started to leave with his men.

Tickory's last words "more money" caused a memory jog for Lord Raisinkatz. After a moment's hesitation, he called after Tickory: "Try Castle Bonjour and Castle Bon Appetite. Drain the moats and look for an iron box in back of the castles."

Tickory stopped his horse and pondered the directions. A smile flickered across his face as he said, "If I am successful, my lord, I will be very obligated to you for this information. Keeping my job means keeping my head, and keeping my head on my body is rather important to me."

Lord Raisinkatz grinned back, "I'll remember what you said, Tickory."

44

"We're experiencing difficulties with our land," stated Na-Nicky the Huntsman one morning.

"What kind of difficulties?" asked Queen Gwyn-o-cheri. She was eating breakfast with everyone, including Lord Raisinkatz.

The huntsman sighed, "Our neighbors. They're doing everything from poaching our fish and game to taking our land and building on it."

"But they know better than that!" argued the Beggar-King.

"They say they can't tell where our property lines are because our fences are broken down. But they simply move our fences wherever they please anyway."

"Which neighbors dare do this?" inquired Lord Raisinkatz, his suntanned face turning dangerous colors.

"All of them. Especially Castle Bonjour and Castle Bon Appetite," reported the huntsman.

"I can send them packing with a few tricks again," suggested the Beggar-King.

"True," said Lord Raisinkatz. "But you can't be everywhere at once. This requires some law enforcement and protection which the king has a duty to uphold." Lord Raisinkatz smiled as he spoke so knowingly about royal policy.

"The Supreme King is too busy fighting his wars. He doesn't care and they know it, so they're taking full advantage of us," said the huntsman.

"We need some sort of guard to boot them off our land and to continuously patrol our forests and streams." Lord Raisinkatz struck one of his favorite poses, lifting one hand in the air while the other pointed downward. "AM I BEING HEARD? IS ANYONE LISTENING TO ME?"

It was the behavior of the Lord Raisinkatz of old, re-born!

Queen Gwyn-o-cheri remained silent. She didn't wish to encourage Lord Raisinkatz's behavior of shouting and demanding, so she waited for another proposal of action from the others.

The huntsman was solemn as he sat with his hands under his chin. "There is no way, short of forcing them off, which means fighting, that I know. If we ignore this stealing of our land and food, soon they will declare that everything we have belongs to them."

Olivia growled, "I'd like to see them try that!"

"I'd like to see them try that!" echoed Jasper, leaping to Olivia's side, his claws showing.

"There's a way," claimed Lord Raisinkatz. "It requires some devious and clever trickery that only I excel in. Let me think. Oh, how easily such methods flicker and flit through my mind." Lord Raisinkatz bent down and whispered loudly, "Yes, it involves some favors owed me by the king's emissaries—such as Tickory Tettle. If you would so allow me the authority to contact them?"

"That would be wonderful," chimed Queen Gwyn-o-cheri. Her smile lit the room like a thousand candles. Her eyes sparkled like the early morning dew on a thousand golden flower petals. Her voice tenderly touched all the living creatures like the warmest of warm sunshine.

The Beggar-King's jaw dropped open. But, for once, no one noticed except Jasper who merely sighed deeply, taking no action.

As for Lord Raisinkatz, his demeanor changed to that of knights of yore. His chest went up and out so far that it almost touched his chin. His spine cracked with the sudden straightening of posture. His heels clicked together loudly.

"I PROMISE TO SOLVE THIS FOR YOU!" he shouted. "IF NOT ONE DASTARDLY WAY, THEN SURELY ANOTHER. LEAVE IT TO ME." Then, as an afterthought he added, "ALL OF YOU AGREE THAT I HAVE YOUR PERMISSION TO DO WHAT IS REQUIRED?"

"Yes," urged Queen Gwyn-o-cheri.

"Yeah," gurgled the Beggar-King, his jaw still open as his eyes stayed on the queen.

"Let's hear the plan first," suspicioned Olivia.

"The plan first!" echoed Jasper.

"WELL NOW," noted Lord Raisinkatz, twirling around and around with his one hand in the air, and pointing his finger downward with the other. "THIS MAKES MY BLOOD CIRCULATE AND IT LOOSENS THE COBWEBS OF MY BRAIN. HOW I LOVE INTRIGUE AND DASTARDLY DEEDS, ESPECIALLY DURING THE DARK OF THE NIGHT OR THE FULL OF THE MOON."

"Or the light of the day," observed Olivia dryly. "You revel in that type of thinking anytime!"

"TRUE. BUT IT SOUNDS BETTER WHEN I SAY SUCH THINGS ARE DONE DURING THE DARK OF THE NIGHT. HMM, I SHOULD HAVE ADDED RAINY—"

"We're waiting," interrupted Olivia. "Tell us what you have in mind."

"NOTHING!" proposed Lord Raisinkatz, but then he reconsidered his proposal. "ON THE OTHER HAND, PERHAPS I WAS TOO HASTY IN SAYING NOTHING. WAIT A MOMENT. LET'S SEE. JASPER AND HUNTSMAN, COME HERE. I'LL HAVE YOU CARRY A MESSAGE TO TICKORY TETTLE. COME HERE, I'LL WHISPER IT TO YOU."

"Why whisper? Why not tell us all?" asked Olivia.

"DON'T YOU KNOW? DON'T YOU UNDERSTAND? THE MOST SIMPLE WORDS BECOME FAR MORE MEANINGFUL IF YOU WHISPER THEM TO ANOTHER PERSON, ESPECIALLY IF YOU WHISPER THEM IN FRONT OF OTHERS."

Lord Raisinkatz laughed as he leapt into the air with happiness. He, Lord Raisinkatz, was once again in charge. It was even a little earlier than his well-laid plans called for. What was more important—he, Lord Raisinkatz, was needed!

45

During the next fortnight, Lord Raisinkatz made appointments to meet with many people. It was clear that he was enthralled with this new authority.

It was like watching a hidden flower suddenly burst forth from beneath the dark, fallen timbers of the forest. Or like a bird that just discovered it could sing for the first time. Or like a little child who just discovered how to talk and now was forming one word after another. Or it was like . . . well, Lord Raisinkatz bloomed, if not quite like a flower, then something close to a flower anyway.

Some of the lord's meetings lasted into the night. But before the castle closed up and the lamps were put out for the night, Lord Raisinkatz insisted on being walked around the outside of the castle grounds, accompanied by Sergeant Muster-Buster and two guards.

Each time, after his inspection, he would enter the large room next to the entrance door and shout loudly so all and sundry could hear, "SKULL-DUGGERY VANQUISHES ALL!" After which he would sing softly:

"Skull-duggery
Hum-buggery
Con-nivery
Con-spiracy."

He then did a small jig as his feet moved happily to an imaginary tune. "HOW DELICIOUSLY HAPPY I AM!"

He continued loudly. "MY MONEY IS GONE. MY WORRIES ARE GONE. MY ILLNESSES ARE GONE."

Then, and only then, humming to himself, did he go to his chambers and thence to bed.

"I think I preferred him the other way," observed Olivia one evening after having watched Lord Raisinkatz from the upper balcony. "At least then, we knew what we were dealing with."

"Why are you so suspicious, Olivia?" wondered Queen Gwyn-o-cheri. "He has changed for the better and helps us keep our land boundaries."

Na-Nicky the Huntsman added, "Well, just last week, the Bonjours came and apologized for intruding upon our properties. They even made payment in goods for their 'temporary' use of our land."

"What about all the animals and fowl they killed?" asked Jasper. "They conveniently forgot about that. You were the one who was the angriest, Huntsman."

"That I was." The huntsman became thoughtful. What Jasper had said was true. Their neighbors had been quite sly about stealing game from their woods.

Trying to change an unpleasant subject, Queen Gwyn-o-cheri asked of her husband, "How are your studies going?"

Before he could reply, Olivia asked, "Who does he meet? What are those long conversations about?"

"Where?"

"Here, there, everywhere. Yes, especially here!" reported Olivia.

"Who are you having these conversations with?" asked Queen Gwyn-o-cheri, looking hurt at her husband.

"I know nothing about this."

"Not him," Olivia remarked. "I mean Lord Raisinkatz!"

The Beggar-King looked from his queen to Olivia. "Do I get to say something or reply to any of this?"

"No, unless you know who Lord Raisinkatz meets with in the evenings," retorted Olivia, sticking out her tongue.

"Olivia!" admonished Queen Gwyn-o-cheri. "He can say and do as he pleases and when he pleases." She strolled over and threw her arms around the Beggar-King whereupon, as usual, his jaw dropped open and the deep red flush, which went from his face to his scalp, straightened his hair, as it too began to change color.

"This gets so discouraging. You'd think, by now, he'd either have an antidote to drink or have something to wire that dumb jaw shut," prescribed Jasper, watching the queen and his master.

Whack!

Jasper went rolling over and over. The kittens squealed with delight and joined him by jumping on top of his belly.

"I must say," observed Jasper after picking himself up and carefully placing himself far away from Olivia.

"The speed and quickness of your paw are most commendable."

"Admirable is another word that comes to mind," added the Beggar-King. "But does it do you any good?"

"Hah! The jaw closeth, the brain worketh, and the voice box soundeth. My master hath returneth to life!" Jasper began imitating his master's opened and closed jaw, mocking the paralysis.

Pow! Slam! Bam-bam-bamity-bam!

In a split second, Olivia had flown through the air and had cuffed Jasper over and over.

"You will *not* set a bad example for our children! Your manners are atrocious. Shame on you for making fun of your master."

"I'm sorry," wailed Jasper, for the blows really did hurt.

All the kittens were delighted at this sport. Each began to cuff the other, saying "Not! Not! Not!" and "Shame! Shame! Shame!"

The huntsman cleared his throat for attention. "Is it agreed that Lord Raisinkatz has helped us and that we should be grateful for his assistance?"

"Hardly," murmured Olivia.

"Yes, I think he should be thanked," agreed the queen. "I intend to do so in the morning."

46

A year went by slowly and during this time, Lord Raisinkatz's health had improved so completely that everyone accepted it. No longer did they comment about it.

Many soldiers came openly to call upon Lord Raisinkatz. Tickory Tettle became a regular visitor and stayed longer and longer with fewer and fewer of the king's men. The knights who did accompany him were now most respectful to Lord Raisinkatz.

Tickory listened more than he spoke, even though no one knew what they were saying which made it a strange set of affairs. Olivia had tried in every way possible to hear their conversations. But the visitors were on their guard to avoid talking, except away from prying eyes and ears, and that included Jasper and especially Olivia.

One day, however, Olivia finally overheard a conversation. "I knew it!" she exclaimed to Queen Gwyn-o-cheri. "He's up to no good. NOW IS THE TIME. Those were his words—he's about to get rid of us and return to power!"

The queen refused to believe it. "Why, I met with him just this morning. He greeted me with such happiness and joy that my heart went out to him. He's a changed man and enjoys everything so much. Why, yesterday he grafted more of the fruit trees that produced the largest apples and pears we have ever seen. He won a prize for his roses. He's growing the largest pumpkins."

"I know, I know," nodded Olivia. "It's spooky."

"He has donated all his prize money and food to the

people. He has changed into a wonderful person. Doesn't that impress you?"

"No! They're just tricks. You'll see. He's full of tricks and these must be among his best."

"Olivia!"

"Tricks. Watch. You'll see."

They saw Lord Raisinkatz approaching them.

"AH! THERE YOU ARE," he greeted them. "I MUST BE AWAY AS DUTY CALLS ME FOR SEVERAL WEEKS. WILL YOU SEE TO IT THAT MY GARDEN PROJECTS ARE KEPT UP PROPERLY?" He handed a list to Queen Gwyn-o-cheri.

"Why, of course, Uncle. It would be a terrible waste to ignore all the work you've done. Besides, I'm anxious to see how these turn out."

Lord Raisinkatz smiled at these words. "YES, I THOUGHT YOU WOULD. PLEASE TAKE SPECIAL CARE OF THE NEWLY GRAFTED ROSE. THE ROOT STOCK IS STRONG AND I BELIEVE I CAN PRODUCE A DEEP, RICH LAVENDER FROM CROSSING THE RED AND BLUE SPECIES."

Olivia sniffed. "So the time has come to take over, has it?"

Lord Raisinkatz was startled. His eyebrows shot up and his brown, garden-sunned skin turned pale.

"HOW—?" he started to ask.

"Cats don't change color," interrupted Olivia sharply.

"AH-HAH!" spoke Lord Raisinkatz with relief, realizing that Olivia was just fishing and actually knew none of the details of his travel plans.

"So you're making your move, are you?" Olivia tried

to continue, realizing she missed her target.

"LET'S SAY MY PENETRATING INSIGHT AND KNOWLEDGE. NO, LET'S SAY MY WISDOM AND FORESIGHT. NO, NOT GOOD ENOUGH. LET'S SAY I PLAYED THE GAME THEIR WAY AND DUE TO MY PHENOMENAL ABILITIES TO ADAPT—"

"You out-connived someone," Olivia interrupted again in her matter-of-fact voice.

"SKULL-DUGGERY
HUM-BUGGERY
CON-NIVERY
CON-SPIRACY."

After Lord Raisinkatz sang his song, he did a quick jig, using just his feet and keeping his upper body steady. "I DID THEM ALL AND I HUMBLY ADMIT I WAS SIMPLY SUPERB!"

With that, he laughed merrily and sang good-bye to the two females as he went out the front door. "GOOD-BYE-E-E-E."

"He's so happy," beamed Queen Gwyn-o-cheri.

"IT'S ALL IN THE CHROMOSOMES!" shouted a voice through the partly opened door. They heard footsteps happily dance away.

"He certainly believes in inheritance. You must be a terrible disappointment to him in a way," pointed out Olivia.

"Oh, there are different ways to achieve something," acknowledged the queen. "His way is not mine."

"Of course, it isn't!" Olivia exclaimed. "He's a male. Males have to fight and shout and carry on with an enormous waste of energy. As he says, it's in their chromosomes."

"Yes, there may be something to that," agreed Queen Gwyn-o-cheri. "But we won't know until someone discovers such things and that might be several centuries or more."

47

"An invitation! Why, that's on my birthday!" smiled Queen Gwyn-o-cheri.

"Interesting why our Sovereign would pick that day," wondered Olivia. "Perhaps it has a meaning and, then again, perhaps not. It does mean, however, we must wear our best clothes."

"It will be hard to get my husband out of his comfortable clothes. He hates dressing up," Queen Gwyn-o-cheri reminded herself.

"He'll learn."

Just then, the Beggar-King and the huntsman entered with a large catch of fish. They were joking and laughing.

Queen Gwyn-o-cheri waved her husband over and showed him the invitation.

"Oh, blast it! That's your birthday," noted the Beggar-King. "We had planned something special for you and it's ruined. I don't suppose we can get out of this?"

"Not a special invitation like this. Never!" scolded Olivia. "It was hand-delivered by a maiden-of-the-court."

"Oh, double blast then!"

"You remembered the date of my birthday," cooed Queen Gwyn-o-cheri softly. She put her arms around her husband's neck and nuzzled, nibbled, and snuggled against him.

"Oh, blast! There goes that jaw again," said a voice that could only belong to Jasper. But he was out of sight.

Olivia, sharp-eyed, looked around the room. "Where are you?" she asked angrily.

"Where you can't find me," chuckled the voice, coming from a different direction.

"I don't see a thing wrong with nuzzling, nibbling, and snuggling!" Frustrated, Olivia stalked around and around.

48

On her birthday, Queen Gwyn-o-cheri and her husband the Beggar-King, Na-Nicky the Huntsman, Olivia and her husband Jasper Bartholomew arrived at King Dinwiddley's Castle.

The castle was decorated with festive ribbons and flags. Knights were standing row after row, and an honor guard was lined on both sides of the entrance to greet the invited guests. The animals on which they rode were taken away to be watered, fed, and brushed. Man, woman, and beast were honored with such warm hospitality for this festive occasion in the royal castle of the Supreme King.

As the guests approached the ballroom, trumpets sounded to welcome them to the large banquet hall. Walking over the threshold, they heard the trumpets sound again, only this time blaring twice. Someone of most importance was about to enter.

All heads and bodies turned, ready to bow down in obeisance, waiting for the entrance of the Supreme King and the Supreme Queen.

What? What was this? Lord Raisinkatz?

Lord Raisinkatz was walking into the large banquet hall with the king's crown on his head! And behind him Tickory Tettle!

Where were the Supreme King and the Supreme Queen?

Why, they were following Tickory! And wearing ordinary clothes! How common they looked.

Lord Raisinkatz walked up to the king's chair. And he even sat down on it!

"YOU MAY APPROACH," he announced in an imperial voice to Queen Gwyn-o-cheri and the Beggar-King. Seeing Olivia move forward with them, he commanded, "NO, NOT YOU, YOU CLOUD-COLORED CAT!"

Olivia growled and hissed under her breath, but remained where she was. Jasper paid no attention and leapt onto the arm of the king's chair. He crouched down, unseen.

"I AM NOW THE KING OF THE REALM! AM I NOT?" Looking around at the massive ensemble, Raisinkatz cued, "YOU MAY SPEAK. I GIVE YOU PERMISSION."

It was the same old Raisinkatz, acting the same old way, as he did before, in the greatest stone castle on top of the highest hill where Queen Gwyn-o-cheri now reigned.

"You are the King of the Realm!" chanted everyone together.

"I PREFER YOUR VOICES A LITTLE LOUDER," he decreed.

"You are the King of the Realm!" the people shouted louder.

"MUCH BETTER," praised Raisinkatz. "THAT HAD MORE CONVICTION."

Raisinkatz stood up, placed both hands in the air as

though he were touching the sky, and cheered himself loudly. "LONG LIVE KING RAISINKATZ!" he shouted to the heavens.

"Long live, King Raisinkatz!" echoed the people.

He lowered his arms and raised his eyebrows. "NICE RING TO IT, THAT! THE WORDS ARE SO CONCISE AND SO MEANINGFUL!"

"And so undeserving," sneered Jasper. King Raisinkatz turned to find that black cat sitting next to him the same old way, as he did before.

"Let me guess," added Olivia, having moved within

speaking distance. "You were the one who sold all the goods to the king, to the former king, that is. At higher and higher prices until you had so much money that you could hire your own army of soldiers."

"WELL STATED, LITTLE TARNISHED CAT."

Olivia snarled but decided this was not the time or place for attack. She would have her day. For now, Olivia was seeing how all the pieces fit together for Raisinkatz.

"So that's why you had all those secret meetings and were sending out so many messengers."

"INDEED!"

"So you gave King Dinwiddley loan after loan. When he couldn't pay, and while his soldiers were away and there was no one to guard his castle, you foreclosed on the loans. He was so vulnerable that you marched in with your own bought-and-paid-for army."

King Raisinkatz's face lit up with a bright smile as it always did when he felt he was being terribly clever. He wiggled in his chair with a joy that trickled up and down his spine. "COULDN'T WE SIMPLY SAY THAT I MADE HIM AN OFFER AND HE DIDN'T REFUSE IT? AFTER ALL, NO ONE TWISTED HIS ROYAL ARM TO SIGN FOR THESE LOANS."

"The offer was probably for him to give in or go to the royal dungeon," said Olivia dryly.

"NEVERTHELESS, HE MADE THE WISE CHOICE. WHAT'S MORE, HE WAS SPARED THE TERRIBLE *Z AND T* 's." Turning his attention away from the cats and toward Tickory Tettle the Tax Collector, King Raisinkatz continued, "I SHALL BE AN EXTREMELY GRACIOUS KING, HAVING LEARNED A GREAT DEAL ABOUT THE COMMON MAN AND HIS COMMON PLEASURES. WHAT SAY YOU, TICKORY?"

"A superb king, your Highness."

"THOUGHTFUL, KIND, AND CONSIDERATE IN EVERY WAY, WOULDN'T YOU SAY?"

"Most thoughtful, most kind, and most considerate," agreed Tickory.

". . . IN EVERY WAY?" added King Raisinkatz.

"In every way," echoed Tickory, his face reflecting a glow from his rare smile.

"DON'T YOU AGREE?" King Raisinkatz looked at Queen Gwyn-o-cheri and the Beggar-King for approval.

"Are you going to tax everybody as you did before?" questioned Olivia. "No one liked you back then."

"BE CHARITABLE, LITTLE WHITE TALKING CAT. I LEARNED A GREAT DEAL SINCE THEN. I'M A DIFFERENT MAN." Then, as an afterthought, he added, "WILL ALL OF YOU COME AT LEAST ONCE A MONTH AND ADVISE ME ABOUT MY BEHAVIOR?"

They looked at each other. Did he mean it or was this just another one of his devious ways to get everyone's cooperation? All agreed to visit Raisinkatz who was now the Supreme King of All the Kingdoms. That is, all agreed except Olivia, who wisely kept her thoughts to herself.

Then everyone cheered because King Raisinkatz told them to cheer. "Hip-hip-hooray!"

And they laughed because King Raisinkatz told them a joke and said it was funny and they should laugh at it. "Ha-ha-ha! Ho-ho-ho! What a funny joke."

Finally, he told them to dance and have a good time, so they danced and had a good time because King Raisinkatz told them that they were to have a good time. "What a good time we're having!"

"THIS IS THE WAY LIFE SHOULD BE!" exulted King Raisinkatz, happily watching the dancing, the laughter, and the cheering.

Queen Gwyn-o-cheri, the Beggar-King, Na-Nicky, Olivia, and Jasper gazed at one another in wonder.

Had he really changed? Or was he just playing games again?

One thing for sure, their lives were heading towards quite an adventure if King Raisinkatz was going to rule all the kingdoms in the entire realm!

About the Author

Harry Chinchinian enjoys writing and illustrating stories for his seven grandchildren. His interest in storytelling and cats goes back to his own childhood.

For over 30 years, the author has practiced medicine and was an associate professor at Washington State University.

He lives with his wife Mary above the Snake River, along with two Irish Wolfhounds and many horses.

This is a story about a beautiful princess who was kind, sweet, and in love. She lived in the greatest stone castle on top of the highest hill.

Along came the musical, magical beggar, looking for his cat, but found the princess and fell in love.

Design and Layout by Matt Gravelle